THE
SPIDERWEB
TRAIL

About the Author

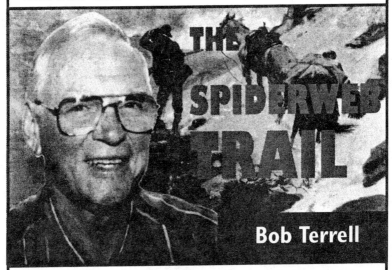

Bob Terrell's love of the West began in his youth, reading Western novels and watching Western movies. He liked the clear-cut difference between good and evil. Although his native North Carolina, where he worked forty-five years as a journalist, is far removed from the West, he has nevertheless maintained a close contact with that part of the country through his life.

He spent two years in California and Nevada, and lived six months in a tent in the Nevada desert writing about the explosion of eleven atomic bombs. Numerous research trips to the West have provided material for this and other novels. He is now working to complete a Western he began more than forty years ago in that desert tent.

A resident of Asheville, North Carolina, Terrell travels frequently to the Middle East as a tour director and has roamed deserts extensively there, particularly the Sahara, the Jordanian, and the Sinai.

In a 1949 interview with Cy Young, the winningest pitcher ever in major league baseball, the twenty-year-old Terrell was advised by Young to make a career of sportwriting. "You'll never find a more exciting life," Young said, and Terrell answered, "Well, sir, I'd rather be writing Westerns."

When his first Western, **The Reluctant Lawman**, was published by Avalon Books in 1991, Terrell had already written 30 books of humor, biography, travel, and music, and several for evangelist Billy Graham.

THE
SPIDERWEB
TRAIL

Bob Terrell

ALEXANDER
Books

a division of Creativity, Inc.

WESTERN ADVENTURE

Publisher: Ralph Roberts
Vice-President/Publishing: Pat Hutchison Roberts

Cover Design: WorldComm®
Cover painting detail adapted
from *Meat's not Meat 'Till It's in the Pan* by Charles Marion Russell, 1915

Executive Editor: Vivian Terrell

Editors: Gayle Graham, Pat Hutchison Roberts

Interior Design and Electronic Page Assembly: WorldComm®

Printed in the United States of America

10 9 8 7 6 5 4 3

Library of Congress Cataloging-in-Publication Data

Terrell, Bob
      The Spiderweb Trail / Bob Terrell.
          p.   cm.
      ISBN 1-57090-022-1 (alk. paper)
      I. Title.
      PS3570.E67748S67   1995
      813'.54--dc20   95-16879
                                        CIP

Alexander Books—a division of Creativity, Inc.—is a full-service publisher located at 65 Macedonia Road, Alexander NC 28701. Phone (704) 252-9515 or (704) 255-8719 fax. For orders only: 1-800-472-0438. Visa and MasterCard accepted.

Visit us on the internet at http://www.abooks.com.

The gloom of early evening arrived on the New Haven Green ahead of John Quay who noted by his pocketwatch that the time was five past five when he took a seat on a bench. Robert Murphy's note asking Quay to meet him here at five o'clock had contained a hint of urgency if not of alarm.

Quay swept the Green with his eyes but Murphy was not in sight. He looked eastward toward the Quinnipiac, flowing silently toward Long Island Sound, and saw traffic increasing as New Haven's laboring population began to make its way home from work.

The air was cold, though not uncomfortably so, but Quay suspected that the temperature had dropped below thirty-two for snow had begun to fall. At first the flakes were small and scattered but as the minutes passed they increased in size until huge, soft, fluffy flakes began to cover the snow already on the ground with a fresh new layer.

Quay had worn a sweater, a short corduroy jacket and a scarf. He tugged his cap down over his forehead and looked at his watch again. Five-twenty. He wished Murphy would hurry but his friend was almost always late.

"Quay," called a voice from behind and John Quay stood and turned to see his friend astride a beautiful gray horse on the edge of the green. In his hands were the reins of a saddled black horse. "Come," said Robert Murphy. "Let's ride around the Green."

Robert was smartly dressed in a tailored topcoat, riding boots anchored firmly in his stirrups, and on his head rested the largest hat Quay had ever seen him wear. Quay knew that beneath the topcoat Robert would be wearing his monogrammed Yale sweater.

Smiling, Quay hoisted himself into the saddle and side by side he and Murphy rode around the edge of the Green, alternately walking and trotting, enjoying the soft plop of huge snowflakes on their faces.

They were of similar height, about six feet, and each weighed perhaps one-eighty. Quay noted that Robert, like himself, had probably not gained an ounce since their undergraduate days when they ran the football for Yale College. He couldn't help smiling at the way the two of them had made the fellows from both Princeton and Harvard yell "Uncle!" on more than one occasion. Both men were trim, athletic in appearance, and handsome, and they struck figures astride the powerful horses that made more than one female passerby turn her head and stare in appreciation.

After their first turn about the Green, Robert pulled in the gray to a steady walk and Quay hauled down the black beside him.

"Where did you get the horses?" Quay asked.

Murphy laughed. "From a stable near where I'm staying."

"And the hat?"

"It's from New Mexico. I bought it in New York."

They rode on for a few minutes and Murphy turned away from the Green and headed east. Weaving their way through a stream of carriages and hacks and hurrying pedestrians, they came to the river. Quay never ceased to marvel at the beauty of the water. Often in his undergraduate days he had come here with academic uncertainties and walked silently along the docks until his thoughts straightened out. More recently, as a student at the Yale School of Law he had spent less time strolling by the river because of the press of his studies.

Now, with the powerful horse prancing beneath him, Quay felt some of the twenty-seven years melt away from his soul, and the exuberance of extreme youth returned. He could see by the set of Robert's shoulders that the same thing was probably happening to him.

Both were sons of wealthy Virginia families and both had been graduated in the same class at Yale five years earlier following glorious careers on the gridiron and acceptable if not spectacular success in the classroom. However, life had not been exactly kind to them since. Quay had returned home and pretended to read law at his father's firm in Arlington, and Murphy, continuing to live with his family in Richmond, had made no progress at all toward a career.

Quay had dropped his reading of law and worked at various jobs around Richmond. Four years after graduation he had assessed his life and concluded that he was making no progress in earning his own way in the world or in finding a wife and settling down to raise a family.

That's when he decided to return to Yale and enroll in Law School. With the excellent instructors at Yale to help him, perhaps he could find more interest in the law away from his father. He had written Robert who, also at loose ends, had agreed to join him in the pursuit of further studies.

So far, Quay's marks had been good and he knew he was making acceptable progress toward a degree in law, which he would receive after another year in school, and that pleased his father tremendously, though it did little to boost Quay's own ego. Still, in five years he had found nothing to do that he liked better than law. He looked upon it as the lesser of evils; he had found nothing, nor thought of anything, that he'd rather do.

Darkness fell while they trotted along the docks, but they had no trouble seeing their way. A lamplighter had preceded them, touching fire to gas lamps which glowed beautifully through the falling snow, as did the windows of buildings along the way. Too, those who were leaving work at this late hour, six or better, Quay guessed, had lighted carriage lamps before leaving.

Robert approached a twin-masted schooner standing at a wharf and pulled in on the reins of the gray, bringing the steed to a halt. Similarly, Quay stopped his mount beside Robert's and for a few moments they watched burly longshoremen loading cargo aboard the schooner.

Robert swung off his horse, and holding the reins, took a seat on a bale of cloth that the workmen were progressing toward. Quay also dismounted and tying reins to a postring, joined Murphy on the bale.

"Beautiful evening," Quay said and Robert nodded agreement.

"Likely we'll get a few more inches of snow before morning," Robert looked upward into the swirling flakes, and

Quay thought something was strange about his friend this evening. Robert's voice carried no mirth, no eagerness, none of the traits that were usually there.

Robert unbuttoned the heavy topcoat and flung it open, revealing the "Y" on the front of his sweater. He remained quiet, as if waiting for Quay to continue the conversation.

But Quay, too, was silent for a time, preferring to watch the muscular, cursing, longshoremen struggle to move dollied cargo up the gangways and down into the holds of the schooner. On the ship's bridge, a flurry of movement in a lamplit cabin beyond mahogany rails, indicated that departure was imminent, possibly within the hour, for the remaining cargo on the wharf had been considerably thinned.

A stevedore, sweat glistening on his brow beneath a warm toboggan, approached them and grinned, "Begorra, lads, ye'll have to move in a minute so we can attack them bales ye're roostin' on. That is, less ye'd rather grab a dolly an' help us out, in which case ye'll only have to move yer horses."

Quay and Robert laughed and stood, and Robert said to the stevedore, "I'm thinking I'd be happier if I took you at your word, but I suppose we'd better be off. Thanks for the offer, anyway."

Quay studied his friend sharply for a moment and then moved to take the reins of the black. He mounted a moment before Robert swung aboard the gray, and together they turned the horses away from the wharf and onto the street, heading again for the Green.

Minutes later, they trotted onto the Green and Robert pulled up and dismounted. Tying his reins to a lamp post, he took a seat on a nearby bench. The glow from the gaslight illuminated Robert's face and Quay read trouble in it as he took a seat beside his friend.

"You're troubled, Robert," Quay said. "What's wrong, my friend? Does that hat have anything to do with why you wanted to meet me?"

"You're right," Robert said, attempting to smile but not quite pulling it off. "I am troubled. And, yes, the hat does have something to do with it. I felt like chucking it all and taking the dolly from that stevedore. I could help them load the rest of that cargo, hide on board the schooner, and by daylight be well away from my troubles."

Quay looked back toward the docks where he could make out no sign of the schooner nor of other ships being loaded, but could see only a dim glow through the falling snow. "That might give you a temporary escape," he said, "but it wouldn't solve your problems, whatever they are."

Robert laughed again, still the hollow, empty, mirthless laugh, and turned sober eyes on Quay.

"I feel like getting drunk," he suggested. "Come, let's find a tavern and have a glass of ale."

"Well, I could go with you," Quay said, "but you know I don't drink."

Leading the horses, they walked through the snow and within a block of the Green came to the Boar's Head. Raucous laughter and loud music sounded within.

"This is as good as any," Robert said, tying his reins to a hitch rail. Three other horses stood at the rail, hipshot in the falling snow.

"Rough-looking place," Quay said, tying his horse beside Robert's. They pushed through the door into a room so filled with smoke they had trouble making out the features of men across the room.

The tavern was filled with roughnecks from the docks. Several glanced toward the door as Quay and Robert entered, but their gazes wandered back to the grog they drank.

Robert ordered a tankard of ale and Quay declined the bartender's questioning look. "Nothing for me," he said. "I'm with my friend here. He'll do the drinking."

Making their way to the back of the room they found an empty table and sat down.

Quay came immediately to the point. "Tell me what's bothering you."

"It's just me," Robert said, looking away as if trying to escape his own thoughts. "I can't really find myself."

"Come, now; that's too vague," Quay said. "Tell me specifics. Maybe we can handle them."

"I'm twenty-six years old," Robert said, "and I have no earthly idea what I want to do with myself. Nothing appeals to me. I've tried working at this and that, and nothing suits me. I don't want to spend the rest of my life being a failure."

"You aren't a failure," Quay said. "You haven't failed at anything yet. You haven't really tried anything."

"I have, too," Robert shot back. "I'm failing in my studies here. We still have another year to go in Law School and I'm failing. At the end of this term they wouldn't dare let me back in school."

9

Quay was thoughtful. "That bad, huh? Well, you must concentrate and pull your marks up to passing. It isn't too late."

"I can't do that," Robert said. "I don't have the interest. I'll never be a lawyer, and it was silly of me to try. I don't even want to be one."

Quay was silent. He had no answer for that.

"I've been thinking," Robert continued, "and there is something I want to do. But I'll have to have your help. I don't want to try it alone."

"What is it?"

"Promise you'll help me."

"Of course, I'll help you if I can," Quay said. "What do you want to do?"

"I want to go West!"

"What?"

"West!" Robert said, and for the first time that evening Quay heard enthusiasm in his voice. "Colorado or New Mexico. Maybe Arizona. Somewhere in the wide open spaces."

"So that's what the hat is about. What do you know about the West?" Quay asked.

"Not a lot, but I do feel it's a place where I might find some answers to the things that bother me. I've been reading up on the West and I'm fascinated with it."

"How can I help you?" Quay asked. "You don't need any money."

"No, not that," Robert said. "I want you to go with me."

"How could I do that?"

"We can leave as soon as school is out in June," Robert said, "and have three months before you have to return."

Quay noticed the drop from plural to singular for the return trip but let the remark slide. "I'm afraid that's out of the question," he said. "I can't go West. I have too much to do here."

"Drop it," Robert urged. "Drop whatever you're doing and let's go. It'll be the best thing we've ever done."

"How is this going to help you solve your problems?" Quay asked.

"Don't you see, I need to get away," Robert said, "away from everything and everyone — except you, of course. We've always gotten along, Quay; I don't think I could go without you. I'd be afraid I couldn't find my way around."

"How in the world could I help you find your way?"

"Just by being there," Robert said. "I need to get away and clear my head, get my mind on something else, forget all this, forget Yale, forget the law. I know I can find my answers out there, but I can't go alone. And I can't stay home. Say you'll go with me."

Quay hedged. The thought of going West had never crossed his mind.

"We could get a job on a ranch," Robert said. "Or driving a wagon. I hear wagon-drivers are in demand."

"You can't drive a wagon," Quay said, "and neither can I. I've never driven a wagon in my life."

"We could learn."

"But I don't want to drive a wagon," Quay said. "I'm studying to be a lawyer."

"I know that. But this will be the best thing either of us has ever done. I just know it will. You could use the diversion from your own studies."

Quay tried to pull from memory the things he knew about the West, and his thoughts came up empty. About all he knew was that the West lay beyond the afternoon sun, in that general direction. Beyond that, his mind was blank.

"This is hare-brained," Quay said. "I can't go West."

"Yes, you can. You must. You can't imagine the country out there: the scenery, the high mountains, the broad valleys, rivers so wide you couldn't swim across them."

Quay admitted to himself that the idea was sounding better. Robert painted a vivid picture.

"There's another reason I couldn't go," Quay said. "I don't have the money."

"Your dad will give it to you," Robert said. "And if he won't, I will. Money isn't the problem. Come on, partner, let's go West!"

Robert's enthusiasm was becoming infectuous, but Quay knew he should continue to resist.

"No. Don't resist," Robert said. "I'm not going to take no for an answer. At least sleep on it and we can talk about it again tomorrow."

Quay saw in that a possible avenue of escape. "All right," he said, "tomorrow."

"Same time, same place," said Robert, finishing his ale. "I'll bring the horses."

"You're talking about the park, not this place," Quay said, and when Robert nodded, Quay affirmed, "Done."

Across the room a trio of ruffians had been getting louder

for a few minutes, and when Quay glanced in their direction he saw they were looking at the table at which he and Robert sat. More precisely, they were looking at Robert's ten-gallon hat.

"Oh, no," Quay thought and for a moment he shut his eyes, hoping the thugs would be gone when he reopened them.

But they were not.

One of the ruffians whispered something to the other two, and the three roared with laughter. Robert also noticed that they were looking at him.

He shrugged. "It's this hat," he grinned. "Let's get out of here while we still can."

They rose and walked to the bar where Robert paid the tab and when they turned toward the door, they saw that they would have to walk by the table occupied by the three ruffians who were still looking at them and laughing.

Quay brushed past the table, and as Robert walked by one of the rowdies stood up suddenly, blocking Robert's path.

"Lemme try that hat on," the ruffian said. "Let's see if it fits." He stepped toward Robert and reached for the hat as the other two came out of their seats.

"Keep away," Robert cautioned the man. "Keep your hands off the hat."

"Hey, Faub," the drunk said to one of the others, "Mama's boy don't want me to touch his hat."

Faub laughed. "Touch it anyhow," he said.

Faub was a brute, more than two hundred pounds packed onto a frame two inches shorter than six feet. The man confronting Robert was tall and muscular, though not as robust as the other. The third man was small, and Quay paid him little mind; he had his eyes on the shorter, stockier, more powerful brute.

The man reached for Robert's hat and with a striking swiftness Robert buried his fist in the man's stomach. The thug doubled over and began to retch, finally going to his knees.

"Here," said the shorter bully, "you can't. . . ."

He had no time to finish the sentence. Quay hammered a strong right to his jaw and sent him reeling into the next table.

"Watch it," shouted a man at the other table, grabbing his overturning stein.

Robert stepped past Quay and blocked a punch from

the third man and then knocked him into the sawdust on the floor.

The short bully recovered and charged Quay, butting him in the stomach and driving him backward to the dirty floor. Unencumbered by a topcoat as Robert was, Quay leaped quickly to his feet, smashed a hard right to the bully's stomach and crossed a left to the jaw, staggering the man, and before he could recover Quay was on him again hammering blows to the body, followed by a hard right to the head. Down the bully went, and the men from the overturned table joined in.

One grabbed Quay from behind and another aimed a right fist toward his stomach, but Quay, locking his own arms around the man behind him, lifted his feet and kicked the oncoming assailant in the face. The man behind him turned Quay loose and Quay wheeled about and staggered him with a left-right combination.

Three others charged him and he kicked hard at them, stopping their charge and knocking one over a nearby table. That table's occupants leaped to their feet and began to fight anyone in reach.

In a moment the entire tavern was up and swinging, shouting, cursing, screaming, mauling each other.

Quay fought his way through the crowd to Robert's back, spun him around and shouted, "Get out of here!"

Robert laughed and swung at a ruffian bearing down on him, chopping the man to the floor before Quay shoved him toward the entrance.

Next thing they knew, they tumbled through the door into the snow. Quay looked at Robert, who was bleeding from a gash above his eye. Blood also poured from Quay's nose and he grabbed a handful of fresh snow and buried his nose in it, glaring at Robert.

"Get the horses," he shouted above the bedlam crashing through the tavern door. "Let's get away from here."

He staggered after Robert, who tore the horses' reins from the hitch rail and flung himself into his saddle. Quay leaped aboard the black and slammed his heels into the horse's flanks. They clattered down the street and around a corner and as they fled Quay heard a policeman's whistle behind him. He urged the black to greater speed and looking back saw Robert, bent low over the gray's neck, hammering his heels into the horse's sides.

In a few moments they were beyond the bedlam and

the falling snow closed in around them. They rode on in half a hurry until Quay pulled up at his own quarters and dismounted.

A light from inside the boarding house fell upon the snow at his feet. Robert also dismounted.

"You'd better have someone look at that cut," Quay said, examining Robert's head more closely.

"It's nothing," Robert said. "It even feels good. At least, the fight felt good."

Gingerly, Quay felt of his own damaged nose and wished it felt as well as Robert's gashed forehead. He laughed softly.

Robert grinned. "You handled yourself well."

"I've been in tougher football games," Quay said, suddenly feeling better himself. "We did give those blokes a working over, didn't we?"

Swiftly, Robert mounted the gray, tipped his big hat, and moved away, leading the black horse Quay had ridden. He stopped and looked back at Quay. "You'd better practice your horseback riding."

"Didn't I ride well enough?"

"Oh, you're a great rider. You'll just have to ride a lot to get your backside toughened up. Everywhere we go out West we'll have to ride horseback."

"I can handle that."

"You might also do some target practicing," Robert advised and touching the gray with his heels he galloped into the night.

Quay wondered why he should target-practice; he had no intention of shooting at anything. He turned his eyes toward the river and thought he detected through the thinning snow the movement of lights on the river beyond the docks, perhaps the schooner plying downstream.

He sat on the steps and for a while enjoyed the falling snow, running his thoughts back through the years. He and Robert had known each other almost ten years, since enrolling as freshmen at Yale, and their paths had been almost inseparable for four years. Then for a few years they were apart, but always in communication, and finally they had come back to school together again.

He liked Robert. No, his feelings were more akin to love. Robert was the brother he'd never had. He felt Robert would do anything he asked him — so why shouldn't he do the same in return? Why not go West with Robert? Maybe he could help his friend find his way.

Quay really had nothing to do this summer. He had no special interest in girls. He had dated a lot of girls but not any of them stirred him enough to make him dream of a permanent romance. He knew Robert had no close ties, either — not even with his family. Quay came from a close-knit family in which each member cared for every other member with a love that was hard for Quay to describe. Actually, he thought, it needed no description; he accepted his family's unity without thought or demand.

"Why not go west?" he said aloud, suddenly realizing that he could think of no reason to refuse, and then to himself he added, "I can get the money from Dad. He'd probably like me to make the trip."

As he walked into the house, closed the door behind him, and headed for his room, he added another thought, "I'll tell Robert tomorrow that I'll go. And tomorrow I'll have to start reading up on the West. I don't want to be taken too much by surprise."

By George, it was hot! How hot it was, John Quay had
no idea, but it must be a hundred-ten degrees or
more. Heat radiated from the rocks around him, rising from the ground to burn his face under the wide brim
of the sombrero he had long since grown accustomed to
wearing.

He wondered who the George was by whom he swore
and concluded that it must have been either George Wash-
ington or King George of England. He made a mental note
to check it out in the Yale library when he got back to school
in the fall and then laughed aloud at the point to which his
intellect had degenerated in the past month.

Nothing in his planning for this trip to the West had
prepared him for the blistering heat of New Mexico. He
had planned as thoroughly as possible for one so ignorant
of a new territory. Nothing he had studied at Yale had mentioned excessive heat.

He could not understand how the cowboys he had met
could cover themselves so completely with clothing in their
efforts to hide from the heat. It was his theory that the
fewer clothes he wore, the cooler he would be, but the theory
didn't seem to work. He'd been laid up three days recover-
ing from a bout with the sun in which he had stripped to
the waist and ridden no more than five miles. At the end of
that distance, he would have sworn he had eaten steaks
cooked no more than were his shoulders and back. Had he
not reached a ranchhouse in the desert where he was taken
in and treated for sunburn for three days, he knew he might
have died.

The brassy sky showed no clouds, nothing but broad

sunshine beating down relentlessly. Thinking back, Quay believed it had been three days since he had seen a cloud, and that only a wisp of cirrus in the western sky. What he wouldn't give for a good Virginia summer shower!

He'd had a bellyful of heat, and as soon as he found Robert Murphy, he intended to talk him into returning to Virginia. Coming West for summer vacation had seemed the thing to do when Robert dreamed up the idea and Quay agreed to it. And his parents had readily agreed to finance the trip. Their reasons, he thought now, had had to do with his maturing. He was physically mature, strong as an ox as he had proved many times in football and boxing at Yale. He knew that Robert was the better football player because he put heart and soul into roughhousing on the gridiron, while he himself had always been secretly squeamish about hitting too hard for fear he would hurt someone. Even with that stigma pestering him, he had been Yale's strongest runner, for he was swift and capable of darting here and there. But he knew that his father never regarded him as being mentally tough enough to cope with the world, despite what he could learn at college. "A summer in the West ought to give the lad a lot of something he didn't get at Yale," he had overheard his father tell his mother.

After a month, he felt no tougher mentally than he had before he left Virginia. The shirt and jeans he wore, and even the sombrero, were beginning to appear worn and faded by the merciless New Mexican sun. Even the expensive, high-heeled boots were beginning to show the wear and tear of his ordeal. So his clothing began to match his attitude toward New Mexico: He wanted to be rid of them at the soonest.

The storekeeper from whom he had purchased his outfit had insisted he buy a used .44-caliber revolver and a hundred rounds of ammunition. The weapon was a big, bulky Colt in excellent working condition. The man said this part of New Mexico still contained a number of desperate characters, any of whom would gladly rid an unarmed man of his possessions. "If my boy was out in a strange land alone with scoundrels runnin' loose," the storekeeper had said, "I'd want him armed." The man was correct, Quay reasoned; it had only been six years ago, in 1879, that the bloody Lincoln County Cattle War had ended in New Mexico, not far from where he now rode.

In Santa Rosa, a sleepy little town with a Spanish accent, he had seen evidence of the storekeeper's cautions.

Watering his horse at the trough in the center of town, having arrived for the first time only minutes earlier, he was suddenly disturbed by a shout, and when he turned to see who shouted, he saw two men approaching each other in the street with six-shooters drawn. One raised his weapon suddenly and let fly, and his three shots kicked dust around the other's feet. Calmly the other lifted his heavy six-gun and shot the first man between the eyes. One shot. The man looked around the street and Quay was the only person he saw in the open. He grinned and tipped back his sombrero with his gun barrel, and said, "Ah, *amigo*, he was a very poor shot, yes?"

Wide-mouthed and staring, Quay realized the man was speaking to him and he shut his mouth, then nodded his head and said, "Very poor, indeed."

"He will no longer have to worry about his shooting," the vaquero said, and holstering his gun, he walked away.

As soon as he reached his horse, Quay had packed the heavy pistol, wrapped in its gunbelt and holster, in a pocket of his large saddlebags, and had not handled it since. An excellent rifle shot, he was not on familiar terms with sidearms and had always been a little afraid of them. But he hadn't seen a desperate character yet; he hadn't passed that many people on the road. Some of the country he had ridden through, would unhinge the average mind. There were canyons and badlands behind him that he wouldn't have believed existed, country torn up and standing on end. He had ridden past boulders larger than houses back home, and some of the country gave him the creeps. Any part of it, he thought, could hide any number of desperadoes and wild animals; though, recalling his ride, the only animals of any sort he had seen were cattle and occasional horses, and there was one rattlesnake resting in the shade of a rock upon which he wanted to sit. But after the reptile buzzed a warning he left the rock to the snake and rode rapidly down the road.

All day yesterday and all of this morning he had ridden a road that lay no more than a mile away from an escarpment on his right. He had never seen a land more rugged, more broken, nor indeed more beautiful. Almost every color imaginable lay in the striated face of the rimrock — magenta, gray, yellow, blue, all shades of red, purple — and at places the rimrock reared more than a hundred feet above the surface of the plain. Clumps of trees appeared back against the rimrock and cattle crowded around them, not as much for the shade, Quay suspected, as for the water that apparently lay in pools within the trees. Waterholes, he had heard them called.

All he wanted to do was find Robert and head for home. He felt quite sure that Robert would feel the same way. He thought he should be nearing the crossroads town of Reynaldo.

So far, Robert Murphy had led him on a wild goose chase. His letter, written two months before, had instructed Quay to come to Santa Rosa and take the stage north to Las Vegas and there he would find his friend; but upon his arrival in Las Vegas he had found a message for him at the post office telling him he would have to come south where he would find Murphy in the town of Reynaldo.

He was now four weeks in transit. He had been so long on the back of a horse that even his saddle sores had saddle sores. At night when he camped, beside a stream when he could find one, he discovered by their soreness muscles that he had never dreamed he had. Usually, he just stripped off his clothes and sat in the cool streams, letting the current massage aching muscles.

He was also about to starve to death. Never before reaching New Mexico had he ever had to prepare a meal, and he had not gotten the hang of cooking his food tastefully.

He didn't know why Robert Murphy had come on ahead, but Robert had dropped out of school in early May and headed west. The three letters John Quay had received at Yale from his friend painted such glorious pictures of the West that Quay found himself most eager to board the train in early June and catch up with his wandering friend.

Catching up, though, had become an ordeal.

He felt certain that somewhere around the next bend, or the next, he would come up with Robert Murphy and the worst nightmare of his young life would soon come to an end.

Quay's father had seen fit to give him enough money to handle emergencies. He had purchased his tickets, his outfit and a rawboned horse in Las Vegas and had enough money in his pocket to see him through another six months or more. But a month from now he expected to be back home on his father's estate in Virginia, ready to face the world.

He rounded a bend in the trail and saw in the distance a town that he took to be, or at least hoped was Reynaldo, a collection of adobe structures that would hardly pass for a slum back home. Heat waves rose and danced before his eyes, widening and stretching the images of the scattered buildings of Reynaldo. Grubby as the town appeared from that distance, John Quay looked upon it with such a feeling of relief that he kicked the horse in the sides, attempting to urge it to a faster gait, but the pony, resisting such foolishness in the heat of the day, crow-hopped across the road with such stiff-legged determination that Quay was forced to drop the reins and grab the saddlehorn to keep from plunging into the dusty road. When the horse saw that Quay was making no further effort to increase their speed, he settled down and moved on at a slow walk toward Reynaldo.

With the town still a mile or more away, Quay saw, off to his right atop a low rise, a lone shade tree. The coolness beneath its leafy branches was too much for him to resist and he spoke softly to his horse, "Gee, boy," and reined the animal toward the tree. Possibly also noting the presence of the tree, the horse increased his gait and Quay approached the shade almost at a trot, bouncing and swinging in the saddle until he thought the jolting might break his neck.

It was only when the horse reached the tree, a rather large and shady cottonwood and moved under its welcoming shade, that Quay noticed the cemetery behind the tree. There were perhaps three dozen graves, some marked with inscribed stones, others with simple wooden crosses to record the last resting place of some of New Mexico Territory's venerable citizens, and several without any markings at all. Two graves near the tree were fresh, their dirt still tumbled and unpacked by rain and weather. A crude wooden cross marked the nearest grave, but was too far for him to make out its wording. The other fresh grave was as yet unmarked.

Dismounting, he slipped the girth of the saddle to give the horse a breather. He sat with his back against the tree trunk, fanning himself with his hat. From his shirt pocket he fished a sack of smoking tobacco and a pad of cigarette papers and rolled a lumpy cigarette. Licking the paper, he sealed and smoothed it the best he could, then twisted one end and put the other in his mouth. Lighting the twisted end, he drew the smoke deeply into his lungs and sighed. A nasty habit, to be sure, but what else was there to do out here? Remembering the canteen tied to his saddle horn, he pushed himself to his feet, secured the canteen, and tasted its tepid water. The alkaline taste made him want to spit it out, but he swirled it around his mouth and finally swallowed it, almost gagging. That was another thing about this country: He hadn't tasted water since he left Virginia that would match the well water at home.

He looked at his half-smoked cigarette, frowned, knowing he should quit tobacco this instant, and flipped the butt into the graveyard.

The cigarette landed in a patch of dried grass at the nearest fresh grave, and in a moment a wisp of smoke curled up from the grass. Mumbling, Quay got to his feet, opened the squeaky gate, and walked into the cemetery. He crushed out the cigarette beneath his heel and stomped the grass around it until he was sure he had eliminated the danger of fire, and as he turned away, his eyes fell upon the crude wooden cross on the new grave.

He stopped, bent closer, and suddenly paled beneath the tan of his face. His heart thumped with a surge of genuine fright, and his knees turned to water. He had to support himself by grasping the top of the cross to keep from falling.

Using a red-hot running iron, someone had printed on the crossbar the words: *Robert Murphy — Too Young To Die.*

Quay staggered out of the cemetery, forgetting to close the gate behind him. He remembered to tighten the saddle cinch and lifted himself into the saddle. Blindly, he turned the horse and pointed him toward Reynaldo. Looking backward at the grave as the horse moved away, he thought by the appearance of the mound of dirt that it couldn't be more than two or three days old.

Surely there was some mistake. Robert Murphy dead! If true, this was a contingency for which he was totally unprepared. What would he do?

What had happened? How had he died, if indeed he was dead at all? Surely this was a cruel hoax, a joke being played upon him. But who would do such a thing? And then it occurred to him that it could not be a joke because the cemetery was hundreds of yards off the road into Reynaldo and no one could have known he would be coming this way. It must be true! Robert Murphy was dead!

Reynaldo was twenty miles from nowhere. It stood baking in the sun a few miles west of the Pecos River. Around the town lay parched rangeland, and he figured several ranches shared the graze, judging by the brands he had seen.

On closer view, the town itself presented a better face than it did from a distance. It had its cantinas, a couple of stores, a saddle and harness shop, a livery stable, two law offices, he noted, and several other shops which attended those who worked in the cattle industry. A stage line was headquartered in an adobe room at the edge of town with plenty of space for stables and corrals, and he saw that it was an express shipping station. Reynaldo was strictly a cowtown with a Spanish taste.

Passersby standing in the shade of store porches watched Quay ride into town at a trot and could not help but notice his demeanor. He wore the pallor of death, and his eyes darted wildly here and there. He almost ran down a woman crossing the street. She jumped and exclaimed, "Look out!"

He sawed back on the reins, almost standing the horse on its hind legs, and the woman swung her parasol at him.

"What are you trying to do," she shouted, "kill me?"

"I'm sorry!" he exclaimed, piling off the horse to stand before her. "I'm truly sorry. I beg your forgiveness, ma'am, but I've just learned that my best friend is dead and I'm looking for the sheriff. Could you direct me to him?"

She noticed the shock in his features, and being at least a quarter of a century his elder, she moved to grasp him by the elbow, for he appeared ready to fall on his face. "You poor boy," she said. "You look a fright. Over yonder. . ." she pointed toward a small but substantial adobe structure on the side of the street she was crossing, ". . .is the deputy's office. May I help you over there?"

"Thank you, ma'am," he said, politely, trying to smile but not quite pulling it off. "I can make it all right."

He led his pony to the building and tied him to a hitch rail. Boots thumping loudly on the boardwalk, he opened the door and entered the office.

A man sprawled in a chair, his feet resting on a desk, hat comfortably covering his face.

Quay cleared his throat and the man woke up, shoving the hat back on his head and thumping his feet to the floor. He was an older man whose killer mustache was graying, partially covering his sunken cheeks. His piercing eyes seemed to penetrate Quay's thoughts, and he heaved himself to his feet, emptied a chair of several newspapers, and said, "Sit down, young man, sit down. I'm Deputy Frazier. What can I do for you?"

Quay slumped in the chair and fought back tears that began to well into his eyes.

"Here, here!" the deputy said, pulling a whiskey bottle from a desk drawer. "Here, man, take a pull on this."

Quay pushed the bottle away. "No," he said. "I don't drink. I'll be all right. Give me a moment."

He composed himself and sat straight in the chair.

"My name is John Quay," he said. "I am a student at Yale College in New Haven, Connecticut, spending the summer in New Mexico. I was supposed to meet a friend here. This *is* Reynaldo, isn't it?"

The deputy nodded. "What is your friend's name?"

"Robert Murphy."

The deputy appeared to be momentarily startled, then he narrowed his eyes and looked Quay over carefully. "Your friend is dead," he said softly, his voice filled with sympathy.

"I know," Quay said. "I just saw his grave. It was such a shock."

"Maybe you better try a swig of this," Frazier offered the bottle again. "Just a small one. It'll brace you."

Quay accepted the bottle and took a small swallow. Suddenly his eyes teared over again and he lost his breath. He gagged and coughed, breathed deeply, and slowly calmed.

"My goodness!" he exclaimed.

"You shore enough don't drink, do you?" Frazier asked, but there was no mirth in his features, only sympathy.

"Is that really Robert Murphy in that grave on the hill?" Quay asked when his voice settled down.

"I'm afraid it is," Frazier said. "Least, he carried identification that named him Robert Murphy. From Virginia, he was."

"Yes, he was from Richmond."

"Friend of yours, you say?"

"Yes. And a classmate at Yale."

"Why were you gonna meet him here? This here's a little bit out of the way from anywhere."

"We were going to spend the summer in New Mexico," Quay answered. "He came on ahead a month before school was out. I'm just now trying to catch up with him."

"What can you tell me about his death?" the deputy asked. "Or about the people he came here to see?"

"Nothing," Quay said, looking more closely at the sheriff. "That's what I was going to ask you."

"You don't know anything about why he was here?"

"Nothing at all. He left a note in Las Vegas directing me here. What can you tell me?"

"I'm afraid I can't tell no more than you've told me," Frazier said, wrinkling his brow in puzzlement.

"Then tell me how he died," Quay said. "He was the picture of health."

"Not when we found him, he wasn't," Frazier returned. "He looked like he'd been drug through the malpais."

"What's that — the malpais?"

"Lava beds. Sharp like glass. He was a mess. He'd been drug some distance on a rope apparently, drug by a horse an' rider, or maybe by horses an' riders. Somebody noticed his body lyin' off the road a few mile south of here, down toward the river."

"What was he doing down there?"

"Nobody seems to know. Cowhands found him, roped his body to a saddle, and brought him here. We went through his clothes, found a letter with his name on it and an address in Virginia — Richmond, like you said. We didn't know what else to do so we buried him on the hill."

"When was that?" Quay wanted to know.

"Three days ago they found him," Frazier answered. "Buried him day before yesterday. He ain't good an' cold yet."

Quay winced, and the deputy, noticing, said, "Sorry."

"Can you tell me what he looked like?" asked Quay, not quite wanting to accept Robert's death.

"Shore. Got it writ down here somewheres." Frazier shuffled through a stack of papers on the desk, said, "Here 'tis. Let's see, he was about five foot ten or eleven, weighed maybe a hundred an' seventy-five or eighty. 'Bout your size, I'd say. Hair, brown an' thick an' a little curly. Age maybe twenty-five, twenty-six or seven."

Quay nodded. Such as it was, the description vaguely fit Robert Murphy.

Frazier suddenly stopped reading and frowned at the paper in his hands. "Well, confound me!" he exclaimed. "Says here he'd been shot once in the back an' another time in the head. I didn't notice that when I looked at this the first time. Didn't read it good, I guess. Wouldn't brought him back, nothin' like that."

"Sheriff," Quay said, sitting upright, attentively. "That means he was murdered!"

"I reckon draggin' somebody acrost the desert till he dies means he was murdered, too, son. I know what murder is."

"What have you done about investigating his murder?"

"What have I done? Ain't done nothin'. Oh, I asked around town but nobody knew any Robert Murphy. He was just an unknown kid to us."

"Aren't you going to do anything? Aren't you going to investigate?"

"Reckon I've done all the investigatin' I can do," the deputy pulled a tobacco sack from his pocket and began to roll a cigarette. "Nobody knows him. I don't know who to ask what. Don't seem to be nothin' more I can do. I'll send a report to the sheriff. Don't know nothin' he can do, either. We can't spend all our time trying to find out who killed a stranger. That ain't the only murder we've had."

Quay was shocked. "Not the only one?" he asked.

"Somebody knifed Old Man Titlow to death the same day your friend was killed. He ran the stage station. Found him dead on the floor in his office. He must've been stuck twenty times."

"Is there a connection between the two?"

"I don't know of any. I ain't been able to come up with a thing. Not even a hint of a clue."

Quay pondered that, then asked, "Can you tell me exactly where Robert Murphy's body was found?"

"Shore, I can do better'n that. Fellers that found him are in the cantina across the street." He held the cigarette in his lips, pulled out a big pocket watch and noted the time, squinting through the smoke. "Least they was in there a half-hour ago; so they might still be. Let's go over there an' I'll introduce you. What did you say your name was?"

Quay repeated his name and followed with a question: "Who wrote that report you read to me?"

"Oh, that was Doc Limbert. Reliable old fellow." The deputy stopped on the boardwalk. "Son, before we go, lemme give you a word of advice. Somebody killed your friend for a reason. I ain't seen nothin' like the way he was killed since the war. . . ."

"The war?"

"The Lincoln County Cattle War. You've heard of William Bonney, ain't you? Called him Billy the Kid. An' Pat Garrett?"

"Yes. I've read about them."

"Well, that's the war I'm talkin' about, and a vicious one it was, too. Blood all over the range. Take my advice, kid, an' don't be too nosy. When you find out how your friend died, might be better if you packed it back up the trail, made yourself scarce."

"What are you telling me? Do you know something you're not saying?"

"I don't know nothin' more," Frazier said, "but I do

know that boy was viciously murdered, an' whoever done it done it for a reason. Could be whoever that was might have reason to come lookin' for his friends."

Before Quay could protest, the deputy held up a hand. "Lemme finish. I ain't sayin' you know somethin' that'll get you killed. I'm sayin' somebody killed him for a reason, an' that somebody might just think a friend of his ridin' into town so soon after his death might know the same thing he knew. I don't believe you do, but I been wrong before. You might be targeted for the next shot."

A shudder ran up Quay's spine. "Good Lord!" he exclaimed, and he walked out of the office behind the deputy, deep in thought.

Halfway across the street, Quay heard the strains of a concertina in the cantina. Frazier shoved open the batwing doors and paused to adjust his eyes to the gloom inside the barroom. Stepping in, Quay saw a half-dozen cowhands, three talking at the bar, two others silently slapping cards on a table, and a third with head on arms, sleeping at a table. A bald bartender, robust in the waist, turned his muttonchop whiskers toward the door and saw the deputy and the stranger, and returned his attention to mopping the bar. In a corner, a young Mexican lightly squeezed a concertina, filling the bar with pleasant sounds. Frazier led Quay to the three at the bar.

"Boys," the deputy said, "this here's, uh. . . . What'd you say your name was, boy?"

"John Quay."

"This here's John Quay," Frazier continued. "Quay, meet Curly Ford, Gus Braswell, an' Sheep Callahan. They ride for the Rockin' R down the road a piece." He addressed himself to the cowboys again. "This's a friend of the man you found dead."

Curly Ford offered his hand. "Sorry about your friend," he said. The other two shook Quay's hand and nodded.

"Let's take a table," Ford suggested. "Bring the bottle, Sheep."

Seated at the table, Ford offered the bottle to Quay, who shook his head. "The sheriff made me take a drink of that stuff," he said, "and it darned near killed me. I've come to learn what you can tell me about Robert. Robert Murphy, that was his name."

While Curly Ford poured drinks for himself and his two

28

friends, Quay quickly studied them. Curly was tall, lanky, with thick, curly hair. Braswell would measure shorter than Curly, but was more stoutly and no doubt more powerfully built; and Sheep was aptly named: His hair, almost white, clung to his head in tight curls, resembling that of a sheep. Quay judged Sheep to be no more than twenty-five. He was not an albino, but his hair resembled that of an albino, Quay thought. All three were dressed in range clothing, jeans, spurred high-heeled boots, high-crowned, wide-brimmed hats, and each had a neckerchief knotted about his neck. All wore sidearms. Curly's rested in a holster at his side and the other two had six-guns stuffed in their belts.

Curly broke the silence. "What do you want to know?"

"I don't know, exactly," Quay said. "I guess I want to know what happened to Robert."

"Other than him being dragged behind a horse till it killed him, I don't know anything. Didn't even know his name. We found him a little ways off the road. He was all skinned up and his clothes ripped an' torn. He was a sight."

"He'd been shot twice," Quay said, and the shock he saw on Curly's face was genuine. The other two registered no surprise, and they were non-commital.

"You don't say," Curly said. "We didn't notice that, he was tore up so bad."

"Did you find anything around him, anything that might give a hint of what happened or who killed him?"

"Didn't look," Curly said. "We just loaded him on Gus's horse and Gus an' Sheep rode double into Reynaldo."

"How far away did you find him?"

"From here, maybe five, six mile. Down towards the river."

"He must have had a horse," Quay mused.

"I'd say he did," said Curly, "to be that far away from town, but we didn't see nothin' of a horse. Didn't study the tracks. We just highballed it to town."

Quay felt a sudden anger rising in him, though not toward the cowboys with whom he sat: toward whoever took Robert Murphy's life. To drag a man almost to death and then shoot him was beyond his comprehension. Or was it the other way around? Was he shot first and then dragged? He felt a compulsion to go and see if he could determine which.

"Could you take me and show me where it happened?" he asked Curly. "I'd be happy to pay you."

Curly frowned. "We wouldn't want no pay," he said, "but I reckon we can show you where. We've gotta go right back that way."

"When can we go?"

"What's wrong with right now? We've got to be gettin' back to the ranch before they come lookin' for us."

The three dashed off another round and Curly returned the bottle to the bar. Quay threw money on the bar to pay their bill, and the four walked out, clamping their hats on before they emerged in the sunshine.

"Where's yore outfit?" Curly asked.

"I'm tied up over by the sheriff's office."

"Then let's get crackin'."

Alternately walking and trotting their mounts, the four reached the scene of the murder in a little more than an hour.

"There's where we found him," Curly said, riding off the road onto a flat and pointing to an area forty yards away. "Don't ride no closer. It might spoil any tracks left."

The four dismounted and leaving their horses, walked to the spot, carefully avoiding stepping on tracks. Quay looked around. To the east, hills rose a half-mile away. The land was open to the south and north, and to the west the country, Curly said, became broken a mile away and was little more than an area of scrambled canyons. Badlands, he called it. Beyond the broken land lay the rimrock, and beyond that, the towering peaks of the Sacramento Mountains.

"He was layin' about here," Sheep indicated a spot on the ground.

"Y'know," said Gus, "he must've been shot first and drug here."

"How can you tell?" Quay asked.

"No blood," Gus said. "If they drug him first and shot him here, where's the blood? He must've bled pretty good from that back wound, the way you described it."

"That's true," Quay said. "If he was still alive after they dragged him, and they shot him then, he would have bled a lot."

Carefully, they reconnoitered, studying the ground. This was a hardpan flat, well covered with creosote and brittle bush. Quay looked at the rough shrubs, and some, which he couldn't identify, bore strong needles an inch and a half long. The ground itself was enough to kill a man being dragged over it, gravelly, crusted, sprinkled with jagged rocks. Heat radiated unmercifully from the ground. He shuddered. Poor Robert! What a terrible way to die!

"Over here," Sheep called. "Here's where they drug him in." He pointed to the tracks of a running horse, he said, coming from the south through the brush and stubble. "Brought him from over there." He pointed southward.

"Let's trail this hoss a little," Gus said, and the four walked beside the tracks of the running horse.

"Look'a here," Sheep said, showing Quay some distinct marks on the ground. "This is where he bounced along the ground behind the runnin' horse. Must've been goin' pretty fast."

Quay recognized the marks, all going in the same direction, as being those of a heavy object dragged along the ground. He could also make out the horse tracks when the three pointed them out to him.

"Anything peculiar about the tracks?" he asked.

"No, nothin' I've seen that would help you recognize them again," Curly opined.

"How far do you think they dragged him?" Quay asked.

"Pretty long ways, I reckon," Curly said, "considerin' the condition the body was in. It was some cut up."

"Let's follow a ways an' see," Gus said, starting off again along the tracks.

"Over here's another horse," Sheep called, and Quay looked for a horse.

"I don't mean a horse itself," Sheep said. "I mean the tracks of another horse runnin' about as fast as the one that drug him." He showed the tracks to Quay, who puzzled over them. They ran parallel to those of the first horse. He could see where the hooves dug into the caliche.

"You an' Gus backtrack these," Curly said. "Me an' Quay can foller the tracks of the horse that dragged him."

"Better still," Sheep suggested, "I'll foller these, an' you an' Quay foller the others, an' let Gus scout over on the other side to see if anybody was ridin' along that side."

"Good idea," Curly said. "Gus!" But Gus was already on the way to the far side.

Curly and Quay returned to the first set of tracks and set off toward the south.

Gus ranged a hundred yards, studying the ground, but he returned to Curly and Quay without finding another trail.

"Look here," Curly said. "Danged if I don't believe this is a blood smear on this rock."

Indeed it was, blackened by the sun but still blood, and a bit farther on they found another smear. Gus found a bit of cloth clinging to a manzanita shrub and Curly said it looked like a piece of the shirt Robert Murphy wore.

From their right, Sheep suddenly began to angle in, and noticing this, Curly called, "Be careful. We're comin' to the place where they started from."

"How can you tell that?" Quay wondered.

"Because the trails are comin' together," Curly said. "Stands to reason that rider over there branched away as soon as this feller started draggin' your friend."

In a minute, Sheep was only ten feet away, still following the tracks of the outrider. "Take it easy," Curly said. "Somewhere along here we ought to find where they started."

Soon they came to a clearing in the stubble, dotted only by tufts of buffalo grass, and Gus said, "Here 'tis. This is where they started from."

Even Quay could make out the jumble of tracks. For a long while, the three cowhands moved gingerly around, but Quay remained stationary, afraid he might disturb an important part of the scene.

The tracks covered an area twenty yards wide, scruffing the ground in places where horses' hooves had scrambled to make quick turns and in other places where action was apparently concentrated.

"Here's blood," Curly called, pointing to a splotch of dark, dried blood on the ground. "Dried before it soaked in," he said.

The four studied the place with care, trying to reach conclusions.

"They were having some fun," Curly said. "Your friend was trying to get away from them and they were probably whipping him with ropes, or maybe knives, or something."

"Here's where he fell," Sheep said. "See that knee print. Plain as day."

Quay looked but wouldn't have known it was a knee print. He marveled at the way the three read tracks.

"He must've been drug to death," Gus finally decided. "Ain't enough blood here to've come from a killin' shot. You say he was shot twice?" he asked of Quay.

"Once in the back and once in the head," Quay said.

"Then this ain't from a gunshot," Curly said. "Maybe

he was knifed."

"The sheriff didn't say that," Quay said.

"Didn't have to be a stab wound," Curly said. "They might've sliced him up some, Injun fashion." Quay winced. "Draggin' him through that brush would have covered up any slicing," Curly finished.

They could determine no more than that from the tracks they read on the ground, although they did find several boot tracks going in different directions, some of them scuffed at the edges.

"He was movin' around some," Sheep offered. "There must have been more'n two jostlin' him around. Two hosses wouldn't made this many tracks."

"Let's split up and scout a little wider," Curly suggested. "Look for tracks comin' in or goin' out."

Carefully the cowboys concentrated their attention on the ground. They split up the surrounding space in grids and each searched a grid. Quay saw nothing out of order. He saw no tracks in the gravelly soil. But the others did.

"Couple of riders come in this way," Gus called from the east, and a few minutes later he found the tracks of a running man. Quay could make them out, the boot heels had dug deeply into the ground and the steps were wide apart.

Sheep found where three riders had ridden in from the south and then apparently ridden back that way when the dragging began. And twenty yards to the west of those tracks Gus came upon the tracks of two horses coming in and also going back out again.

"Well, we've established somethin'," Curly said when the four returned the center. "Looks like seven men was after this gent, an' when they caught him an' had their fun, five went back the way they'd come and the other two finished the job. Not much blood here an' not much over yonder where we found the body, so if I was asked to guess, I'd say whoever rode along to the side over there must've shot your friend as the other dragged him. Man on the draggin' horse would've been too busy to shoot."

"Any chance we might follow some of these trails going away?" Quay asked.

"Not much," Curly replied. "After somethin' like this, they'd hide their trails sooner or later."

"One thing puzzles me," Gus scratched his chin. "Where's Murphy's hoss? Surely he wasn't out here without a hoss an' outfit."

"Why don't we go see?" Curly said.

They backtracked the boot tracks, obviously made by Murphy while running from the mounted men. The tracks led eastward and were fairly easy to follow. A quarter of a mile away, Curly suddenly exclaimed, "Huh-oh!"

"What it is?"

"Horse fell here," he said. "An' its rider come up runnin'. Look at this. Here's a spot of blood."

They walked on for thirty yards but found no more boot tracks, only those of a running horse.

"'Pears they might've shot his horse," Curly mused. "Wounded it. Didn't kill it."

"How do you know?"

"It ain't here," Curly looked at him frowning. "Use your head. You're smart enough to figure out some of these things even if you are a tenderfoot. Looks like he rode to here, an' when his horse went down, he ran on afoot, tryin' to get away. The horse got up and went thataway." He pointed toward the northeast.

Quay thought: That's my first lesson in Western lore. I've been taking the tenderfoot approach of ignorance, thinking possibly they do things differently out here, that things don't work as they do back east. But that's wrong. There is no difference. All I have to do is use my brain and think, and if I apply common sense, I'll get along, because that's what these cowboys have going for them: They may be unschooled in books but they have common sense. And they use it.

"Let's look back yonder where we found the body and see if we can find which way them two went after they killed him," Curly suggested, and they returned to the place where they had discovered the body. A while later they found the tracks of the two killers' horses going back into the road.

"Turned toward town," Curly said. "No chance of follerin' them any farther. If they stuck to the road their tracks have been covered up long since. Pretty good traffic on this road."

"We better be headin' back to the ranch," Gus said, pulling a stemwinder from his pocket and checking the time. "It's nigh onto six o'clock."

"Hate to leave you, Partner," Curly said, "but we do have to go."

"That's all right," Quay said. "But if you could do one

thing more for me, I'd be obliged. Give me the lay of the land, where the ranches are located and all."

"Shore we can do that," Curly said, dismounting. He found a long stick and began drawing in the sand.

"This line is the road we're on. Town's up here, an' we're down here. Over here on the east, lined up from beyond town right down to here, are four ranches, pretty good spreads. The first one up there is the Tumbleweed. Feller named Tumbler owns it. Right nice place. He's put plenty money in it to fix it up, an' he's made a right smart out of it. Good graze an' a lot of cattle.

"Next place down is the Lazy G, owned by Britt Garfield. Pretty good ranch there, too. Runs maybe two thousand head; got six, eight hands, countin' the cook, about the same as Tumbler. Garfield never made trouble for nobody that I know of, though I don't know too much about him. Never met the gentleman.

"Then you come to the Willet place. Old Man John Willet and his two boys, Zeb an' Rayburn, run it by theirselves. They ain't as big a business as the other two, an' their place is kept up clean as a whistle. They got too many cows for three to handle, an' the old man ain't as young as he used to be, but he carries a full load. The two boys is hard workers, shore enough; they ain't got time for such shenanigans as this — an' if they did, their pap'd kill 'em for gettin' mixed up in somethin' of this sort."

He paused and started to get up, but Quay asked, "What's the fourth ranch down there?"

"Oh, that's the Rockin' R where we work. We run cows clear to the Pecos; got maybe three thousand head an' ten good riders. If any of 'em are playin' games like this on the side, I shore don't know about it."

"Don't overlook one thing," Sheep put in, "an' that's that this didn't have to be done by anybody from them ranches. Could'a been anybody from anywhere, maybe even some gang that chased him here."

"Correct," Curly said, "but we're just givin' him the lay of the land at the moment. Over yonder to the west there ain't but two spreads, the Hook-Eye an' the Sixty-Eight. Both of 'em are twenty miles away, between the badlands an' the rimrock. Good buffer between them an' the ranches over here. Either one of 'em would make two of any of these ranches east of the road. They're big, maybe five thousand head an' fifteen, twenty hands. The Hook-Eye might even have more."

"They're big," Quay said. "What are they like?"

"Don't know that," Curly said. "None of us has ever been to one of 'em, let alone worked there. They're company ranches, owned by interests back East and operated by ranch managers."

Curly gave some thought to an idea that formed in his mind, and then addressed Quay again. "If I was lookin' for a startin' point, I'd go see Old Man Willet. I wouldn't think for a minute that he or his boys was tied up in this, but he can give you the low-down on everybody on this here mesa. He's been here forever an' knows more about everybody in the country than anybody else I can think of."

"Got the best grub around, too," Sheep laughed. "His daughter cooks for them, and she shore knows what to do with pots an' pans. She's a cooker!"

"Name's Pearl," Curly said, grinning. "She ain't just a cooker, she's also a looker."

"Mighty easy on the eyes," Gus offered. "You go over there, you be careful, boy. If'n they like you, they might rope an' hogtie you fer Pearl."

"That'd be an awful nice thing, if I do say so," Curly said. "You'll know what we're talkin' about when you see her."

The four climbed on their broncs, and the three cowhands headed southeast toward the Rocking R. Quay turned his horse back toward Reynaldo, and when he rode into the street of the town he saw a light coming from the deputy's office window. Tying his horse to the hitch rail there, he knocked on the door.

"Come in," the deputy's voice sounded from inside. "Oh, it's you, is it?" he added when Quay stepped inside. "Figured you'd left."

The words nettled Quay. "A friend of mine has been murdered here, Sheriff," he said. "I'm not leaving until I find out what happened to him."

"Told you everything I know," Frazier said. "Now that ain't much, I'll admit, but it's as much as I know."

Rankled, Quay flared. "You might know more if you looked around."

"Now, what does that mean, boy?"

"It means I rode down to the place Robert Murphy was killed," Quay said, "and pieced the thing together. Part of it, anyway."

"You did that? How?"

"I had help. Those three cowboys you introduced me to went with me."

"Ahuh. They're good men. Figured you might be goin' down there when I saw you ride out of town with them. What'd you learn?"

"First, let me ask you a question. Have there been any strangers in town since a day or two before Robert Murphy's body was brought in?"

"Far as I know," Frazier said, "just you. Might have been others, but I didn't see 'em. I don't see everybody that comes to town."

Quay told the deputy what he and the three cowhands had deduced by reading the tracks at the murder scene.

"Like readin' a book for some men," Frazier said. "I never could make heads or tails out of tracks myself."

"They can. I learned a lot."

"I know they can. Curly's part Indian. Used to be an army tracker. Well, what brings you back to town, son?"

"To ask a favor," Quay said. "I may need some help at times to pull off what I'm going to do, and I want to make sure you're willing to help."

"What are you going to do?"

"I intend to find who killed Robert Murphy, and bring them to justice."

uay spent the night in Reynaldo's only hotel, which was comfortable enough compared with some he had slept in, and when morning came he was ready to ride. Curly had said a good place to start would be the Willet ranch. The deputy gave him directions. "Go east about a mile and when you come to a north-south road, take it south. That'll be to the right. It goes by the Lazy G, and the next place is the Willet spread. House is a mile or two off the road, but you'll see the gate. Ain't hard to find."

He found the road easily. For a while it paralleled the road he and the three cowboys had taken to the murder scene, but the deputy had told him the road he was now traveling turned east again between the Willet ranch and the Rocking R. He had ridden about an hour when he came to a track swinging off the road to the east, and fifty yards off the road was the entrance to the Willet ranch. He pulled up and studied the land, broken in places, lumpy with hills, but it appeared to contain good graze. He urged the horse through the entrance and up the ranch road.

A half-mile in, he topped a rise and saw the Willet spread in the distance. The ranch buildings lay near the center of a mile-wide basin. He saw a house, a barn, scattered outbuildings, two large corrals, but nothing like a bunkhouse because the Willets had no hands except the two sons. What were their names? Zeb and Rayburn.

The ranch buildings were shaded by cottonwoods. A stream tumbled down the basin slope east of headquarters and ran through the ranch yard, its course in the distance marked by green cottonwoods. The far slope was covered with timber, mostly pine, and within the basin lay many acres of rich grassland. Quay knew the Willet holdings reached beyond the basin.

Cattle dotted the valley floor; how many of them Quay could not attempt to estimate.

The ranch road ran from where he sat his saddle straight down the valley to the buildings. Quay nudged his mount into motion and it walked lazily down the road. Before he was halfway to the ranch, he saw a man step onto the porch of the house, shade his eyes from the sun's glare, and look toward him. Another man came out of the barn and also stared toward Quay. He went back in the barn and came out again with a rifle in hand.

Scenting water, Quay's horse broke into a trot, and he let it go, knowing if he tried to check its gait it would probably try to buck him off again. As he rode into the ranchyard, both men approached him, the one with the rifle warily, he noticed.

"Howdy," said the man from the house. "I'm John Willet. Who might you be?"

"My name is John Quay," Quay returned, dismounting. He saw that Willet was tall, perhaps fifty, his hair gray at the temples and salted with white throughout. He wore rough range garb. Quay had dismounted on the off side from the younger man with the rifle, but the man moved around until he could bring the rifle to bear again on the stranger. He did not cover him, but held the weapon loosely in his right hand, the barrel pointing toward the ground.

"This is my son Zeb," John Willet said. Zeb was around twenty-five, tall like his father, and a handsome man, his bearing erect. He nodded without speaking and Quay saw that his eyes were dark and piercing. Undoubtedly, this one would be a fierce fighter, Quay thought, and wondered immediately why he was thinking like that.

"My girl's got dinner on," Willet continued. "Whatever your business is, I'm hopin' you'll stay and eat. We pride ourselves in our victuals and like company time to time."

"Yes, sir," Quay broke into a grin. "I'll be happy to stay. My own cooking's about to kill me."

"Zeb, take his horse," Willet commanded. "Young feller, you come with me."

Zeb shifted the rifle to the crook of his elbow, apparently satisfied that Quay meant no harm, took up the horse's reins, and led it toward the nearest corral. John Willet directed Quay toward the house.

The noonday sun bore down — another hot day, Quay thought — and then they stepped upon the porch and he smelled the cooking. His mouth began to water. That had to be ham frying!

The house was sturdily built of large pine logs, the roof shingled. The porch ran the length of the house, perhaps sixty feet, Quay thought. It was remarkably clean; so were the ranchyard and the outbuildings. The place had the appearance of concentrated care.

Willet opened a screen door and bade Quay enter. He stepped into a large living room, handsomely furnished by a woman's hand. The furniture was smart and, Quay thought, French, though he knew little of such. The room contained none of the stuffed leather chair and dark paneled look that dominated most ranches. Doilies dotted the tables in the room and two vases were filled with lovely cut flowers. Three Winchesters were racked beside the door, within easy reach, but the remainder of the walls were decorated with paintings depicting Western scenery in bright, cheerful colors.

"My daughter's work," John Willet said. "She's a painter of some note, around here, anyway. Gets her paint all the way from Kansas City."

At that precise instant, Pearl Willet entered the room from the kitchen. The sight of her almost took John Quay's breath. Indeed, she was the loveliest girl he had ever seen. A cloud of dark hair, beautifully done, framed a face so lovely that Quay thought it would be impossible to describe. Her eyes were brown, her lashes long, her mouth perfectly shaped and breaking into a smile.

She was tall, like her father and brother, only a couple of inches shorter than Quay's six feet. Her curves were all in the right places and very prominent; her breasts beneath the white blouse were full, and she moved with such grace that Quay was stunned for a moment.

"Honey, this is Mr. Quay," her father said. "Mr. Quay, my daughter Pearl."

"Indeed you are," Quay said, taking her hand and bending low to kiss it.

"Indeed I am what?" she asked, her eyes flashing the smile that had already spread across her full lips.

"A pearl, Miss Willet," Quay said. "You are indeed a pearl of rare beauty."

She blushed and immediately changed the subject. "I'm

glad you've come in time for dinner," she said. "Father, please show Mr. Quay where to wash up. Everything is on the table except the ham, and it's ready."

Willet took Quay out the back door to a porch much smaller than the front porch and indicated a basin already filled with water. A towel hung on a nail beside the basin. The scent of lye soap and dampness permeated the area. Quay washed his hands, then splashed water on his face and rubbed it around, and dried on the towel. Willet followed suit, and as he finished Zeb and Rayburn Willet came around the house to wash.

"Here's my other son, Ray," John Willet said. This one was as tall as the other, rangy, also a handsome young man, and obviously younger than Zeb. He offered his hand, mumbling a greeting, and Quay shook hands.

John Willet led the way back to the table. His broad shoulders were bent from hard work, but the twinkle of youth was still in his eye. He seated himself at the head of the table. His sons took the next chairs, and Quay seated Pearl, then made his way around the table and took the seat next to Zeb.

Quay hadn't seen such a spread of food since he left home. Ham and beef filled two platters. There were bowls of corn, beans, potatoes, tomatoes, and chili peppers, and a platter of cornbread. The Willets certainly ate well, Quay thought. He accepted the bowls as they came around and filled his plate.

"Eat well, young man," Willet told him. "We'll have what's left over for supper."

They ate in silence, Willet and the boys shoveling in the food as fast as they could chew and swallow. Hungry as he was, Quay was not far behind. Pearl minded her manners, eating more slowly, occasionally glancing at Quay. Once their eyes met, and she smiled broadly. He returned the smile and continued to eat.

When they finished, Willet pushed back from the table and looked at Ray. "How're things on the east range, Son?" he asked.

"Reckon they're all right, Pa," Ray Willet said. "The waterhole at Lookout Point ought to be cleaned, I think. Saw some strange tracks east of the spring, but they looked like riders movin' through. Two of 'em. I trailed them about a mile but they didn't stop or change direction. Grass is pretty good for this time of year."

Willet nodded and looked at Zeb. "How're you comin' on that tack?"

"I'll be finished this afternoon," Zeb said. His voice was deeper than his brother's. He appeared to be the oldest by two or three years. Most of the harness is in good shape. Got one saddle that we ought to take to Wilson. Needs mendin'. I'm cleanin' and oilin' everything."

"Good," Willet said. He looked at Quay. "Have to take a day now and then to keep our riggin' in shape. Man can't work without proper equipment, and Zeb here keeps it up."

"Your saddle needs some work," Zeb said to Quay. "I'll clean it up and see if I can fix a place or two for you."

"That's nice of you," Quay said. "I'd appreciate it."

"What brings you our way?" Willet put the question directly to Quay. "We don't get many strangers off the road here."

"I'm looking for information," Quay said, "about a friend of mine. His name is Robert Murphy. I was supposed to meet him here, but it seems someone killed him. I'm trying to find out what happened so I can send word to his folks."

At mention of Murphy's name, the Willet boys exchanged sharp glances but said nothing. Quay was certain Pearl Willet caught her breath, but when he looked at her she was composed and staring at her plate.

"You say he was killed?" Willet asked. "Was he the feller them Rocking R hands found?"

"He's the one," Quay responded. "He was killed on the edge of your range, near the road going south from Reynaldo. It hasn't been a week."

"Heard about it," Willet said, "but I don't know anything to tell you. All I know is what I've heard in town. Buried him there, I believe."

"Yes, on the hill north of town," Quay said. "Hadn't you ever heard of him before? He must have been around a while."

"I. . . ," Pearl started to say something, but her father cut her short. "Never heard of him," he said, staring sharply at Pearl. "Don't believe he'd been around long or some of us would have known him. Heard of him, anyway. You boys know anything about him?" he asked Zeb and Ray. Both shook their heads without looking up.

Quay said. "We were both from Virginia, and were students at Yale."

"Yale College?" the older man asked. "Reckon I've heard of it."

"Yes, sir, it's a known school."

Quay looked at Pearl and she dropped her gaze again to her plate.

"I can't imagine why anyone would want to hurt Robert," Quay said, "let alone kill him. He had never harmed anyone."

"You might check the other ranches along here," Willet said, rising from the table. "They've all got hands, and they'd have more contact in town than we do. Boys," he looked first at Zeb, then at Ray, "back to work. Time's wastin'."

Quay was ushered into the living room by Pearl, who said, "Mr. Quay, how long are you going to stay out here?"

"I don't know," he heard himself say. He was trying to listen to the conversation in the kitchen. "I want to stay until I find what happened to Robert."

He heard the old man say, ". . . fix his saddle and get him out of here."

"Have you a room in town?" Pearl asked.

"What? I beg your pardon; I'm sorry, I didn't hear you," he said.

"I asked if you are staying in town."

"Yes," he replied. "I'm staying at the hotel." He was picking at a broken fingernail, but had nothing in his pockets with which to cut it.

"Pearl!" Willet called from the kitchen. "Pearl, come out here a minute."

She excused herself and left the room. Quay looked around the room and spotted a clasp knife on the mantle. He got the knife and started to open it, but stared at it in his hand and suddenly thought he recognized it. Turning the knife over, he saw the initials R. M. carved in the walnut handle.

"Robert Murphy!" he breathed. "I'd know this knife anywhere." Quickly he placed it back on the mantle. Assuring himself that Pearl and her father were talking in the kitchen — in such low tones that he could not make out the conversation — he moved around the room, seeking other evidence of Murphy's presence. A door stood open to a bedroom and he stepped into the entrance and saw hanging on the front of a clothes bureau a highnecked sweater with a large "Y" sewed on the front.

"That's Robert's sweater," he said, and suddenly fury welled up within him. He strode swiftly across the bedroom, took down the sweater, and carried it into the living room just as Pearl Willet reentered.

She uttered a cry, "Father. . ." and Willet shouldered past her. Quay held the sweater out to them.

"What's going on here?" Quay demanded in his sternest voice. "This is Robert Murphy's sweater! You do know him! He's been here!"

Pearl turned pale and sat down. Her father advanced on Quay.

"What are you doing?" he shouted. "You've been prowling in my daughter's room!"

"I saw the sweater from the doorway," Quay said, his anger reaching the apex. "Robert Murphy has been in your daughter's room. He left his sweater there. That's his pocket knife on the mantle. What was he doing here? Did you kill him?"

Willet stopped in his tracks and looked back at Pearl. Her eyes pleaded with him. "Tell him, Father. Or shall I?"

Willet sat down. "Young man, have a seat," he said. "We have some things to tell you."

"I hope they're good. I'll be riding into Reynaldo to see the sheriff."

"No need for that," Willet said. "Yes, we knew Robert Murphy. And yes, he had been here. He was here not long before he was killed. He stayed here several days, hiding out. I thought he was falling in love with Pearl."

"Did you kill him for that?"

"We didn't kill him. We thought he wanted to marry Pearl."

"I didn't even think about marrying him," Pearl said. "We were friends. It never went beyond that. But I didn't want to see him get hurt."

"He didn't think anybody knew he was here," Willet said to Quay again. "He was trying to hide from some men he had fallen in with. He stayed here two weeks, mostly in the house. He was afraid to go out in the daylight, fearing they might be watching the house."

"Why were they after him?" Quay asked. "What had he done? And who were they?"

"We don't know who they were. He wouldn't tell us. He didn't want to implicate us."

"Implicate? In what?"

"We don't know that. He wouldn't even tell Pearl. He was mixed up in something and didn't realize it until it was too late to get out, he said. He came to us and we put him up. They must have been watching the house, for they came in the night. He went out the back door, managed to saddle his horse, and left on the run. We saw them go after him."

"How many?"

"I don't know. Half a dozen or more. Too many."

"When was that?"

"The night before his body was found."

"Why did he come here in the first place? Did you know him?"

"I met him in town," Pearl said, composing herself. "Ray drove me in to buy supplies, and I met him in the store. We talked, and we were attracted to each other, but only in a Platonic way. He asked if he could come calling, and I said he could. He was a lonely man, and he had been here several times before the last time." She began to cry softly. "I can never forgive myself," she uttered. "It's like I lured him here — to his death."

Quay felt sympathy replacing his anger. "You can't feel that way," he said softly. "You didn't lure him. Anyone would want to follow you."

She looked at him through tear-wet eyes and quit sobbing.

"Didn't he give any hint at all why he was running?" Quay asked.

"Not any," she replied. "But he was running from something terrible. He was frightened out of his wits. He spent the daytime looking out the windows, watching the valley, hoping they wouldn't come. But he said the Indian would find him, that sooner or later the Indian would work out his trail and they would come. And they did."

"What Indian?"

"He didn't say. He just talked about the Indian as if he were a part of whatever Robert was a part of."

"Why didn't you tell me this to begin with?" Quay asked. "Why hide it from me?"

"Mr. Quay," Willet explained, "whoever Robert Murphy was mixed up with are dangerous, desperate men. They didn't give him a chance. We've had no trouble with them; don't even know who they are. We've got a place to run here and, shorthanded as we are, that's tough enough without adding somebody else's worry to it. We mind our own business and sometimes have to look the other way. I've got to think of the consequences for my family. I'm all they've got left since their mother died, and they're all I've got. Beside them, this ranch don't amount to a hill of beans."

"I understand that," Quay said, "but a man was brutally murdered on your range, almost at your doorstep, a man you'd sheltered for two weeks. You can't just ignore that. You can't stick your head in the sand and hide from society. There are times when you have to be a part of it."

"I know that, son," Willet said, "and I know I was wrong to hide it from you. But I was thinking of my family and trying to do what I thought best."

"What kind of horse did Robert have?" Quay asked, remembering that the horse probably had been shot but had apparently gotten away.

"He rode a blue roan," Willet said, "with four white stockings, and a big, powerful horse it was. Had a blaze on its face that looked like a dagger. That's what your friend called his horse — Dagger."

"Have you seen it since?"

"No, we ain't. It didn't come back here."

Quay started to leave, then thought of one more thing and turned back. "What can you tell me about the station agent who was murdered?"

"Titlow? Good, honest man. Family man. About sixty, I'd say. Quiet and neighborly. Never harmed a soul, far as I know. Children grown and married, but his widow lives in town."

"Could you think of anything that might connect his murder to Robert's, even remotely?"

"No, I couldn't. Except they happened on the same day."

uay left the Willet ranch downhearted, trying to treat his thoughts of John Willet with charity. Perhaps it was true what the Indian had said to the white man: You had to walk a mile in his moccasins before you could begin to understand him. He believed the Willets had nothing to do with Robert Murphy's murder. But he had accomplished what he went to the Willet ranch to do: He now had more information about Robert's death.

Suddenly he didn't want to go back to town. He needed time — and a place to think. He had his camping outfit with him, skimpy as it was, but it had seen him through a lot of nights so far. When he was out of sight of the Willet place he turned off the road and headed for the hills. Perhaps up in the timber he could sort out his thoughts and draw a line on what he needed to do next.

Riding a wide circle to the north around the Willet place, he remembered what Ray Willet had said to his father about seeing the tracks of two riders crossing the ranch. When he could, he held the horse to rocky ground, shunning the easier path across grazing land, trying to hide his own trail. Why did he do that? Did he care if the Willets knew he traveled this way? He told himself he didn't care, that he only wanted to see if he could hide a trail.

In midafternoon he reached the forest, climbing steadily, and once in the pines he felt better. He found a game trail and followed it upward. When he came to a small stream he followed it, knowing he would need water for a night's camp.

The mountains were higher than he thought. He knew the mountains to the west of the road reached almost ten

47

thousand feet, but these were less tall, maybe six thousand, he reasoned. Here, though, he could hide and stay a day or two without detection.

Late in the afternoon he came to a small mountain valley, well hidden, with nothing but a game trail leading in. The valley covered no more than two acres, but the grass was good and a small stream ran along the edge by the trees.

"This is good," he said to his horse. "Let's ride once around it and see if anybody's been here." He was eager to test his newly-found tracking skills.

Nothing in the valley, as he circled it, hinted of man's presence. Only then did he decide to camp near the stream. Throwing his saddle and gear, he watered his horse and staked it in the grass on a twenty-foot rope. Immediately it lowered its head and began to pull at the grass. Assured no one was around, Quay made camp and built a small fire, spreading his bedroll between the fire and the trees beside the creek.

He wasn't sure he was still on the Willet ranch. He had ridden upward most of the afternoon and it was hard for him to judge the distance he had covered. He might be on Lazy G property now, but it didn't matter. No one had used this valley in recent times, perhaps never. It was so secluded he was not sure he could find his way in here again. He thought how nice it would be to have a place to get away, and in the endeavor he was currently engaged in, he might need a hideaway. Wouldn't it have been good if Robert Murphy could have found this valley instead of hiding at the Willet place? He might still be alive; he might still be here.

He broiled bacon over the open flame and wolfed it down with hardtack and branch water, then watered the horse again and staked it a bit farther from the fire.

Night fell like a dark blanket. He stared across the meadow and watched the trees on the far side slowly fade away in the disappearing light. Soon he could see nothing outside his firelight except the huge stars above, winking at him like faraway eyes. The night was warm, but a soft breeze crept like a ghost into the valley, stirred the flames of his fire, and went away again. He lay back on his bedroll, laced his fingers behind his head and looked at the stars for several minutes, trying to sort his thoughts.

The first thing he must do, if possible, was locate Robert's horse. Where he found it might give him a clue.

He laughed. A clue? A clue to what? Perhaps to the next thing he could do. He could move only one step at a time. There was no set course of action he could take until he learned more. He tried to think like a detective.

Robert Murphy had been in trouble. What sort of trouble he could not imagine. The Willets said he had been mixed up in something. In what? How could he find out? He didn't even know the country, and he certainly did not know, nor did he understand the people. Too, he had no idea how to go about looking for evidence. "Then I'll just blunder along," he said to himself.

Robert had been associating with the wrong people, that much was clear. Was he in league with a gang? There were at least seven of them. If it was a gang, what sort of gang? What did they do? Hold up travelers or stagecoaches? Rob banks? Rustle cattle? He had heard nothing of illegal activities in the two days he had been here, but that didn't mean there weren't any.

Where should he begin now that he had a bit of information? Maybe he should visit the other ranches and see if Robert's horse had come to any of them. That would be a starting place. But how could he find it if it hadn't?

A final thought drifted through his mind: What was the connection between Robert's death and that of Titlow? There had to be one. The chances of two men being indiscriminately murdered on the same day in a place as small as Reynaldo were remote indeed. Maybe he should talk to Titlow's widow.

The next thing he knew it was dawn. He came out of a deep sleep and saw the trees across the valley taking shape in the early light. His horse roused in the meadow and began to pull at the grass again. Only white ash remained of his fire. He stirred the ashes but they were cold. The fire had been small and of dry wood and had burned away quickly. Using dry wood, he built it again, and went to the creek to splash water on his face. It felt so good he returned to his gear and found a small piece of soap; then he stripped, plunged into the cold water, and bathed. Afterward he led his horse to water, cooked breakfast, and packed up his camp.

Before leaving, he climbed to the highest peak bordering the valley and searched in all directions, but nothing came to eye except more forest. As far as he could see, the woods stretched away empty and silent.

He loved the view, the forest broken by rugged ravines. Instead of going back to the valley the way he had climbed up, he went down the other side of the peak, and halfway down he came to a small bench hidden by pines. On the back side of the bench, small shrubs had caught brush and piled it against the mountain, and for a reason he could not explain he walked to the brush and began poking about. Suddenly he found a passageway and stepped into a depression that led to the mouth of a cave. He looked around and noted that the cave was hidden from view, even from the bench.

Selecting small dry sticks from the brush, he held them tightly in his hand and lighted them with a match. In a moment they flared and he moved inside the cave. Immediately it opened into a sizeable room. The floor was dusty but there was no evidence of tracks, not even animal tracks. The cave was dry and large enough for a man and his horse with room to spare. In the rear, a small opening led farther back in the mountain, but his torch began to dim and he hurried back outside. He would save exploration of the smaller opening for another time, but he filed the location of the cave in the back of his mind and made his way off the bench and down to a game trail.

Immediately he saw the tracks. The game trail was churned by the hooves of several passing horses. Quay could not tell how old the tracks were, though not any appeared to be fresh. Tracks went in both directions.

From the trail back to the mountain valley was a quarter of a mile and the distance was filled with trees. Despite the trail, Quay felt that the valley was still sheltered enough to be considered his secret.

He rode through the trees to the valley and turning in his saddle looked back the way he had come and could make out no sign of a trail.

"Good," he thought. He was not alarmed by the tracks. A lot of people probably passed this way at one time or another.

As well as he could, he followed the stream down the mountain and in a few minutes crossed the creek and picked up the game trail again. He still could see no fresh tracks. When the game trail led away from the stream, he left the trail and rode downward near the water, always keeping it in sight, and the trail always came back to the creek.

He noted landmarks along the way, hoping to return here at times; he really liked the little valley. Often he turned in his saddle and studied the hills behind him, marking certain landmarks in his mind; he would have to remember them from this angle because this was the angle from which he would see them on his return.

It was noon before he broke out of the woods onto rangeland again. Here the graze was good and cattle prevalent. They were big, rangy, rawboned animals with long horns and nasty disposition. He thought they glared at him as he rode past. He noticed no uniformity in color among the cattle. Brown and tan were predominant, but he met one old bull whose hide was yellow as the sun with flecks of white. The bull lowered his head and showed Quay his hornspan and Quay's mouth fell open in surprise. The bull's horn tips were six feet apart, maybe more. Quay kicked the horse in the ribs and left the bull behind before it made up its mind to charge the strange rider.

Here and there were cattle of a rich chocolate brown, and others of purplish hue. Some hides were mouse gray. Since arriving in New Mexico, he had heard horses of that color called *grullas* Many of the steers were dappled with spots of red, blue, or brown, and some were more than dappled: They were decorated with huge, ragged splotches of white on brown, or black on yellow, resembling the pinto ponies he had seen. Most of the cattle had a stripe a shade or two lighter than the color of their hides running the length of their backbones.

Quay marveled at the animals. He saw a half-dozen steers that he swore would stand six feet at the front shoulders, huge, wiry animals with long and skinny but apparently sturdy legs.

The horns on many of the cattle were broken; Quay suspected this was from fighting. Their horns were of all shapes, sizes, and crooks and twists. Few had the same shaped horns.

These were Texas longhorns, Quay knew. He also knew he was on Lazy G range because most of the animals wore that brand. As long as he was this close, why not pay a visit? Maybe he would find Robert Murphy's horse there. From the picture the cowboys drew from the jumbled tracks where Murphy was killed, his horse apparently galloped off in this direction. There were few fences to hinder his progress in a straight line. This country was still largely open range. Herds mixed together somewhat, but the hands on each ranch hazed neighboring steers back to their home range, keeping the herds mostly separated. That was one reason the work of the Willets was so hard and demanding, being shorthanded as they were.

In midafternoon he found the road to the Lazy G and followed it. The ranch's headquarters stood on a knoll with a few trees scattered in the yard at the top of the knoll but none down the sides of the rise. Good field of fire, Quay thought, and immediately wondered at himself. Until recently he wouldn't have thought of a field of fire. Now he found himself looking for such. The Lazy G bunkhouse was larger than the main house, both built of adobe, and Quay did not find that unusual. Britt Garfield was a single man, Curly had told him, and he needed less space than six or eight hands and the cook. There were the other buildings, a barn, outhouses, tool and equipment sheds. As he rode up, Quay saw two mowing machines beneath a tin-roofed shed, and knew immediately that these were used to gather winter feed for cattle.

Two hands walked from the barn as Quay approached the place, and both dropped what they were doing and waited until he rode up.

"Howdy," one of the hands said, shading his eyes against the lowering sun. "Step down and make yourself to home."

"Thanks," Quay returned, dismounting. He offered his hand to the cowboy and said, "I'm John Quay."

"Name's Wayburn," said the other. "Junior Wayburn. I'm foreman here. This's Rooster Red," he indicated the other cowboy, who grinned and doffed his hat to show Quay his brilliantly red hair. Then he threw back his head and crowed like a rooster, prancing in a circle. "He's a pretty good hand," Wayburn said, "when we can tell him what to do. He ain't all there, though. Thinks he's a chicken."

Quay didn't know whether to laugh. Rooster Red was funny. He bounced off toward one of the sheds, scratching himself under his arms and crowing loudly.

"Don't pay him no mind," Wayburn said, chuckling. "He's been that way since he got shot in the head a year or two ago. We didn't think he'd live for a while, but he come around. What can I do for you?"

"I'm looking for a horse," Quay said.

"We got plenty," Wayburn returned. "What did you have in mind?"

"A big blue roan with four white stockings and a dagger blazed on his face."

Wayburn frowned. "That's a tall order," he said. "Does it have to be exactly that? We might be able to find something similar."

"Did you ever see a horse of that description?" Quay asked.

Wayburn scratched his grizzled chin. "Might be," he said. "Young feller in town had a roan matching that description. Saw him a week or so ago."

"That's the one I'm looking for," Quay said, beginning to trust Wayburn. "That young man was a friend of mine, but he was shot and killed a few days ago on the Willet ranch down near the north-south road."

"Ahuh, that one, eh?" Wayburn said. "That's shore a shame. He was a fine-looking feller. Come on up to the cookhouse, and let's have some coffee. I'll answer all your questions I can there."

They walked to the cookhouse and entered the dining area. A long board table stretched almost the length of the room. It had chairs on both sides. Quay counted twelve of them.

"Have a seat," Wayburn said. "I'll get the cook to rustle us some coffee." He went in the kitchen, from which wafted tantalizing aromas of cooking food. Wayburn returned and sat across the table from Quay.

"Tell me about your friend," he said.

Quay told him the story, straightforward, leaving nothing out except yesterday's visit to the Willet place. The cook brought in a coffeepot, two mugs, two plates, and put an apple pie between them. "Might as well sample that," he said. "Be a while till supper."

The pie was delicious and for a few minutes the two ate in silence.

"I'm looking for any kind of information I can get on Robert Murphy," Quay said. "I need to send word home to his family, and I don't know what to tell them."

"How bad was the horse shot?" Wayburn asked.

"I don't really know that he was shot," Quay said, "but if he was hit, it apparently wasn't hard. He ran away and came in this direction."

"He didn't come here," Wayburn said. "And I haven't heard anything of a wounded horse. Course, I ain't been to town in a week, and we don't get much news out here. You think your friend was runnin' with a gang, you say?"

"No, sir," Quay answered. "I think he must have been mixed up with a gang in some way. There were seven riders after him when he was killed. No one can make me believe Robert was part of a gang; he wasn't that kind of person."

"Reason I asked," Wayburn offered, "was because there's been an incident or two north and west of here. Stage holdup couple of weeks ago; man was robbed over toward the Sixty-Eight a day or two later. And then there was Titlow's murder. One of the boys was in town last week and swears he saw the Clodhopper comin' out of one of the cantinas about dark."

"The Clodhopper?"

"People think he's a bandit," Wayburn said. "He's suspected of being a highwayman. Nobody's ever caught him, so he's only suspected. But wherever he shows up, things start happening. Name's Claude Hopper, but everybody calls him the Clodhopper. He runs with a no-good gang, or they run with him. They're called the Clodhoppers, and they hit and run. Small stuff, highway holdups, stage jobs. They leave the banks alone, just hit small stuff out on the road so they can get away fast. If he's around here, you might keep your ear to the ground. He'd be up to something."

"Thanks," Quay said. "I'll remember that."

"Where are you bunking?"

"I'm staying at the hotel in town," Quay said, "and if you hear anything at all that you think might help me, I'd appreciate your sending word."

"I'll do that, you bet," Wayburn said, finishing his coffee. "I've got to get back to work. Why don't you hang around for supper and even stay the night? You can sleep in the bunkhouse. Plenty of room."

Quay suddenly felt compelled to do that. His rear was sore from riding all day. He doubted that he would ever get accustomed to riding long hours every day. Range hands were a gossipy bunch, he knew, and someone might drop information he could use. Too, he could put a couple of good meals under his belt.

"Thanks," he said. "I'll take you up."

"Supper'll be in about an hour," Wayburn said. "You can go up to the house and sit on the porch — Mr. Garfield ain't here — or you can tag along with me and watch me and Rooster work."

Wayburn had been more straightforward with him than the Willets, though he had no ill feelings toward the Willet family for the way they had withheld information about Robert Murphy. He felt Wayburn had given him a clue to the whole affair: The Clodhopper gang would bear investigating. But where and how would he start? With the deputy? He felt Wayburn could tell him no more, but the deputy might. He should be up to date on the whereabouts of a gang of suspected thieves.

He walked to the house and sat in a straight-backed rocking chair on the porch, hoping to straighten out his thoughts and find some answers. As he rocked it occured to him that he was not getting any answers — but the questions were surely piling up.

He dozed in the afternoon sun.

When Quay discovered the secret cave in the mountains, he was four miles from the west entrance to Coldwater Canyon, a deep and beautiful cleft in the hills, two miles long. The canyon floor was flat; in places it measured a half-mile wide, and its steep walls, here and there rising three hundred feet in the air, gave the place an eerie feel.

Coldwater was a badman's paradise, so far removed from the great basin of Reynaldo as to be almost inaccessible. It was seldom visited by anyone who was not on the run from the law. The land was open, unclaimed and uninhabited. Running west to east, the canyon was easily guarded on the west — one good man with a rifle, plenty of ammunition, and a cold eye, could hold off a brigade there — and on the east it led toward the Pecos River and the Llano Estacado, a fearsome high-plateau country of extreme heat and scant water.

Coldwater Canyon was named for a creek of the coldest water in New Mexico that rose from bold springs within its boundaries and flowed eastward along the south canyon wall, to tumble down the mountains and empty eventually into the Pecos. Near the center of the canyon, some of these springs in eons past had flowed with such occasional force that they had eroded side canyons and smaller draws to the depth of the main canyon, as if building extra rooms onto a large house.

The citizens of Reynaldo and other towns within reach of Coldwater Canyon usually left the place alone, trespassing within its boundaries only when necessity demanded, and then with much trepidation and in considerable force of numbers. There were some who believed Coldwater Canyon was the favorite hangout of Billy the Kid when he needed immediate and nearby refuge from the law. No one alive today could attest to the fact that William Bonney had favored the canyon, but that mattered little; legend had a way of growing into truth in a man's fancy.

At one time Coldwater Canyon had been a refuge for marauding Indian gangs who could ride out and strike in force at whatever pickings presented themselves. The location of Fort Sumner a couple of day's ride to the north had ended the Indian problem, but some of the canyon walls were still blackened by the smoke of their campfires.

Coldwater Canyon was a busy place these days. When Quay sat at the front of the cave he had discovered above the beautiful mountain meadow, a dozen men were spending their days working and sweating in the canyon. They slept at night in a camp within a mile of Quay's cave. Their camp was located in a large draw unconnected to Coldwater, with an opening over a ridge to the north for easy getaway. Access from Reynaldo to this home canyon was by way of the trail that passed Quay's cave.

A big, grizzled puncher named Cling was in charge of the cattle operation in Coldwater Canyon, and he ruled it with an iron hand. To expedite the work, he used the services of a roper named Handy Jones, who could, the boys said, rope a rattlesnake in a fast crawl. Handy's rope sang all morning, snagging steers and dragging them to one of two fires burning on opposite sides of the canyon where others heated branding irons to a red-hot degree and reworked the brands on the sides of the steers.

Already, more than three hundred steers wearing the W brand of the Willet Ranch, the Lazy G, the Rocking R, and the Tumbleweed had been roughly rebranded with a WXL. The stench of burning hair caused cowpokes dragging steers to the fire to wrinkle their noses.

Others hazed the bawling, rebranded cattle through a small draw on the south side of Coldwater Canyon into a grassy side canyon large enough to hold several hundred steers.

Most of the work in Coldwater Canyon took place early in the morning after a crew had driven the fruits of a night's labor into the big canyon. These crews picked up cattle in the basin, sometimes by twos and threes, and drove them into the hills to a rendezvous where two men held them until early evening when all hands had delivered their take. The crew then pushed the steers up through the mountains, never using the same trail twice, and by sunup turned their catch into the canyon for the branding crews to rework.

Some of the men were expert hands with a running iron, but in this case the running iron was unneeded. The WXL brand had been devised to fit perfectly over the Willet W, rebranding those steers without visible trace of wrongdoing, but the brands of cattle from the other ranches, including the Hook-Eye and the Sixty-Eight west of the badlands, had to be blotted before the WXL was applied.

Mopping his brow with a huge red bandana, Jim Rafter lifted himself to his feet beside a branding fire and complained. "Pears to me somebody could have come up with a better brand than the WXL to fit over these other brands — somethin' with curls and loops to fit over the Sixty-Eight, the G, and the Hook-Eye in particular, and even the Tumbleweed. We're doin' a lot of extra work here we ought'n be doin'."

"Shut up," Cling commanded, approaching the fire. "Knock off the gab and get back to work."

"Nothin' to do at the moment," Rafter said, "not till Handy drags up some more beef. If you want us to hurry, tell him to rush it up."

Cling turned his mount and rode away, and Rafter, following him with his eyes, said, "I don't see him down on his knees in the dirt, rasslin' with these damned cows."

His companions, Ranny and Joe, stretched their legs, then sat on a rock beside the fire and rolled lumpy cigarettes, lighting them with branding irons.

Still and all, though the work was backbreaking and suffocating in the heat and dust, this job beat the holdup duty this crew had been performing on the roads to the north of Reynaldo. The road agent's life was riskiest of all, and Rafter, Ranny, and Joe hated it. You never knew when a fast man with a gun would be the one you chose to rob and would force the issue before he gave up his wallet. You never knew how many passengers rode the stage you stopped, and you never knew how many of them were willing to open fire as soon as the coach halted, defending their lives and protecting their property.

The sun lipped over the canyon wall, flooding the floor with light, and most of the men began to pack away their tools and catch up horses for the return ride to camp. The rebranding operations usually ended before noon.

The three-mile ride back to camp through the forest was pleasant, Rafter thought, and if you didn't count the morning branding sessions, life here with Garney's outlaw gang wasn't all that tough. The money was good, and Garney paid on time. Every man-jack here was taking in more than two hundred dollars a month, and Garney didn't take unnecessary chances. He never overworked a territory. Likely as not, they would be moving soon, before the valley ranchers began to miss too many cattle. So far, their herds had each been dented only by the loss of perhaps fifty head, and scattered as their cattle were through the valley and in the foothills, it was sometimes hard to miss fifty head from a herd of two or three thousand.

Sam Baines had the pots boiling when the crews came in, and he lost no time dishing out grub for twenty hungry working men. Sam made the best beefstew in the Southwest, Rafter judged. His cooking alone was enough to keep a puncher working with this outfit.

Three canvas tents stood on one side of the draw, used by Garney and his lieutenants. Cling occupied the smallest one.

Sizeable sitting logs surrounded the camp's main fire — not Sam's cook fire — and the punchers brought steaming plates of stew to the logs and sat to eat and talk, griping, complaining, or joking about whatever came to mind.

With his men thus gathered, Cling had only to finish his stew and rise to say, "Boys, we've got to make a drive. We got too many cows penned in that canyon now, so tomorrow at sunrise I want the six men I'm about to name to start that herd out of the canyon, take it back across the Llano, and sell it off to the forts on the plains."

He looked around at the upturned faces and called off six names — "Rance, Bob, Bowlegs, One-Eyed Pete, Dutch Henry, and Charlie. Rance is in charge. Pete will take enough grub for two weeks on a couple of pack animals. You ought to have no trouble. When you get back, we'll have another herd ready to go. Any questions?"

The six whose names were called were pleased. Driving a small herd, even across the Staked Plains, was far superior work to grovelling in the canyon branding cattle. Anything beat that chore.

"What about the Indian?" Rance asked. "He ain't goin', is he?"

"No," Cling said. "The Apache stays here. We got other uses for him."

"Good," Rance said. "I get a spooky feelin' ridin' with him."

The Apache had not been seen since breakfast. He kept his distance from these men, feeling neither affection nor distaste for them. He had no feelings at all, eyeing all others as men who might eventually supply him with things he needed, either willingly or otherwise. To the Apache, it didn't matter. He made no friends; wanted none, in fact, because friends sometimes were cumbersome.

Even Rattler Baines, with whom he usually worked — never on cows, always on people — was not a close friend, simply a working companion as cold as the Apache, never hesitating to kill when opportunity arose or occasion demanded. Baines was the swiftest and deadliest man with a gun the Apache had ever seen, but when it came to knifework, the Indian had no peer. The two made a deadly team.

The Apache seldom slept in camp, but made his own bed higher in the hills. He trusted no one, especially these hard-eyed men who lived on the wrong side of the law. The Apache had no feelings about that. Either side of the white eyes' law was all the same. Among the Mescaleros there were fewer laws and thus fewer things to bind a man's hands when he thought of something unsavory he wanted to do. Let the white eyes live by their laws; the Apache had his own.

A loner by nature, the Apache was still at war with the white eyes, and he was in league with these few only to accomplish his ends. Association with them gave him the opportunity to strike the white man at times in absolute safety, protected by the remainder of Garney's men. But he didn't have to associate with them. He came to their camp only on occasion, to lift a few supplies from the cache of edibles, to replenish his ammunition. When he came he spoke to no one; he took only what he needed and quietly faded into the woods.

Jim Rafter had a bad feeling about this job. No one had said anything or done anything to bring the feeling upon him. He couldn't put his finger on the trouble, but something was not right. The money was good; in fact, better than usual. Each of the men in the camp was being paid ten times more than the average cowpoke's thirty a month and found. He was sure Cling was making more than the others, which was no more than right, seeing as how Cling had the duty not only of overseeing the work but also of running the camp. It was not an easy job keeping this many men in line, Rafter thought, especially when they were men such as these — thieves, murderers, highway robbers.

He couldn't talk to Cling, or Jinglebob McShane, who spent most of his time in Garney's company, or Handy Jones. Not any of them would understand. Sam Baines might, but he was the brother of Rattler Baines, and he might slip and drop a word of their conversation to his deadly brother. He could talk only to Ranny and Joe, his partners in crime for many years.

Ranny and Joe came to the fire and stretched out, feet to the blaze, shoulders resting against one of the logs.

No one else was around.

"Either of you guys know what we're here for?" Rafter asked.

"Huh?" Ranny peered at him.

"I reckon to rebrand a few calves," Joe laughed. "Seems to me we've worked over half the cows in the territory."

"There's more to this job than that," Rafter said. "When I signed on, Garney told me he had a big one in New Mexico and he expected it to pay off like nothing before. Besides," he added, running his eyes over the camp, "look around here. We got twenty men already and more coming. We don't need that kind of manpower for a six-bit rustling operation. Something else is up and I'd really like to know what."

"I dunno," Ranny offered. "Maybe you're right. We do seem to have more men than we need, but I ain't complaining. It's paying right well. I drawed upwards of three hundred last month, and that's more'n I ever made in my life."

"We all did," Rafter returned, "and that's all right. That's a good month's pay. But Garney said there was more to this than that."

"Hmmm," Ranny mused. "Might be that bank in Reynaldo. Looks pretty stout to me, so it must hold a right smart of valuables."

"And money," Joe helped out. "If there's more to this job than helpin' ourselves to the other man's cows, it must be the bank. I bet these ranchers keep it full of money. This is damned healthy stock we're dealin' with."

Handy walked up to the fire and sat on a log. The three ceased their talking. After a minute's silence, Handy asked, "Ain't you gonna cut me in on it?"

"On what?" Joe asked.

"On whatever you're plannin'," Handy said, wiping the back of his hand across his mouth. "You're talkin' awful low, so it must be somethin' big." A beam of smugness crossed his face, as if he'd figured something out that he shouldn't have.

The three laughed.

"What we're talking about," Rafter said, "is how these valley ranchers are going to howl when they find out how many cows of theirs have slipped away."

"Ought to be a sight to see," Ranny joined in.

Handy stood and looked at the three in disgust. "Shore. Shore," he said. "That's all right. Keep it to yourselves. Ole Handy'll find out what you're plannin' to do, an' maybe he'll tell Cling. Might be he just will. So you better watch out."

He stomped away.

"The son of a bitch," Joe uttered. "Somebody needs to shoot him in the back of the head one dark night."

"Why don't you volunteer?" Ranny wanted to know.

"We could make a list of them amongst us that need killing," Rafter said. "What troubles me is that as many as we've got on this job, the world wouldn't miss a one of us, was we to check out. Think about that."

They turned that one over for a moment, and Ranny laughed. "I ain't doin' this for the world. Gimme another year an' I'll have enough stashed away to buy the prettiest spread in Colorado."

"Yeah," said Joe. "That's about as much time as I need. I'm goin' to put so many miles between me an' New Mexico I can't never find my way back."

"We're getting away from the subject," Rafter said. "I still have a bad feeling about this job. Something's not right. It's too secretive. Did either of you ever go into a job and didn't know what was coming down?"

"Not me," said Ranny.

"Me, neither," said Joe.

"Then what the hell are we doing here?" Rafter asked. "I'm half a mind to pull out now while I'm still in one piece."

"You're just spooked," Ranny said. "Maybe that boy got to you last week."

"Could be it," Rafter said, thinking of Robert Murphy flying through the creosote and joshua trees on the end of the rope. "I'm still a mind to pull out." A shudder went up his spine and he shivered.

"What's the matter?" Joe asked, looking at him closely.

"I dunno," Rafter said, throwing a chunk of wood on the fire. "My mother would've said somebody just walked on her grave. I still might get outta this place tonight."

"I can't afford to," Ranny said. "The money's too good."

Cling pushed open the flaps of his canvas tent and emerged into the coolness of the high mountain air. He stretched and looked around camp. Men mending saddles and bridles, cleaning and oiling weapons. Cling's gaze stopped on Rafter, Joe, and Ranny sitting by the fire. He walked to them.

"You three," he said, "saddle up. Time we touched the Hook-Eye and the Sixty-Eight again. Been a couple weeks since we paid 'em a visit. Get on over there and don't come back till you round up a hundred head. You know how to get there and how to get the cattle back. Leave now."

Abruptly, he turned on his heel and walked back to the tent.

"Here we go," Ranny said, heaving himself to his feet.

Joe followed, and the two looked back at Jim Rafter.

Rafter still sat, silently gazing into the fire, deep in thought. Finally he raised his head and looked at his two sidekicks.

"What the hell," he said and rose to his feet. "Like the man said, let's saddle up. We got work to do."

Quay was introduced to the other seven range hands of the Lazy G at supper. Rooster Red he already knew. He met Benny Satterfield, Larry Cook, Arapaho Joe Davis, Clingman Seltry, Hook Nelson, Spider Wellman, and Wayburn's son, Melvin. He liked them immediately — most of them. Davis and Wellman were rather reserved, he thought, quiet, perhaps introspective men, but the others were outgoing, fun-loving practical jokers. All were tanned to a leathery brown by the New Mexico sun, and all were roughly dressed in range garb. As they came in the cookhouse door, they removed their chaps and flung them in a corner, drew back chairs and sat down, and began sniping at the cook.

"Hey, Cookie, what's for grub?" Satterfield shouted into the kitchen.

"Leftovers for you," the cook shouted back. "Beefsteak for ever'body else."

"Hey, I want beefsteak, too," Satterfield said, "and make mine rare."

"Say, I like it rare, too," Larry Cook echoed.

"Not me," said Hook Nelson. "I like mine half rare and half raw. I want it just so's it won't beller when I forks it."

They all laughed hugely until Cookie emerged from the kitchen and stabbed a great butcher knife in the table. He threw a large cooking fork beside the knife and returned to the kitchen to fetch a box of sulphur matches, which he tossed on the table beside the fork.

"Tell you what," he said, "I'll jes' go outside and round up a cow and run her through here and when she passes by, why don't you all just slice off what you want and cook it yersef's with them matches!"

They laughed uproariously, their banter all in fun, but when the cook spread the table with victuals, including a huge platter of steaming steaks, all funning ceased. Eating was serious business with these men, and they conducted their business in silence. Great chunks of beef and bowls of beans disappeared. Never had Quay seen more hearty appetites. These cowboys would make any cook happy.

Later in the adobe bunkhouse, Satterfield, Cook, Seltry, and Nelson went immediately to a lamp-lit table in the center of the one long room and began to play poker with a greasy deck of cards.

The room was about thirty feet long, Quay estimated. There were two windows in the front wall and one at the end of the room opposite the fireplace. Twelve bunks were built against the back wall, leaving no room for windows, but Quay saw three upright slits in the wall, widening toward the interior, that he thought must be rifle ports. Furniture was scanty, a couple of tables and an assortment of chairs. Pegs in the adobe walls held the cowboys' sparce belongings. Three or four chests rested beside the bunks of the better-heeled hands.

"Ain't anybody got a better deck o' cards?" Satterfield asked, trying to shuffle. "These is gettin' so thin you can read 'em from the back."

"You can read 'em from the side, too," Cook interjected, "the way you got 'em thumbnailed. They look like they'd been sliced with a knife."

"Shut up and ante," Hook Nelson joined in good naturedly. "We ain't got all night."

For a while, the slap of cards came from the table, and the men bantered in the cowboy's customary way.

Davis and Wellman sat to themselves on a couple of bunks, quietly discussing something. Rooster Red worked on a bridle, mending a split, and Melvin Wayburn lay on his bunk, dozing.

Quay pulled up a chair and watched the poker game. The stakes were not high, and nobody was a big winner. Similarly, no one was a big loser, and conversation flowed easily around the table.

Darkness drew a black shade over the windows, and now soft snores came from Wayburn's bunk. He was fast asleep.

"Mel must've had a hard day," Cook laughed, looking toward the snoring man. "His daddy gives him the toughest jobs, trying to make a hand of him, I guess."

"Huh!" Seltry snorted. "Can't be nothin' tougher than rousting cows out of the brush. Mel had it soft, if you ask me, cleanin' out that waterhole."

"I'll be glad when we get these dogies rounded up an' counted," Nelson offered. "I can think of a lot better things to do than haze cows outa the brush. Big steer charged me this mornin'. That ol' blue steer with the twisted horn."

"You mean Old Meanness hisself?" Satterfield asked.

"That's the one," Nelson said. "If I hadn't been ridin' Dandy he'd akilled me shore."

"What'd you do?" someone asked.

"Why, after I got out of his way, I threw my rope over his horns and busted his tail a time or two, an' after that all he wanted to do was get away from me."

"Anybody else ride Coldwater Canyon today?" Seltry asked.

"Not me."

"No, I didn't."

"Didn't get near it. Why?"

"Well, I saw somethin' strange up there. Tracks of a half-dozen hosses come down out of the hills to the waterhole in the canyon."

"What's wrong with that? People ride through this country all the time."

"Ain't that," Seltry said. "These weren't ridin' through. They went back the way they come in, drivin' some cows, headed for the flats up there, I'd say."

Quay had Davis and Wellman directly in his vision over the shoulder of Larry Cook, and he alone saw the look that passed between them when Seltry mentioned the riders. Davis furrowed his brow and Wellman frowned deeply when their eyes met. Almost immediately they recovered and quit talking to listen to the conversation at the poker table.

"What would anybody be doin' up there?" Nelson asked.

"Beats me," said Seltry, "but they're up there all right. Six or eight of 'em. I didn't count the tracks."

"Probably a hunting party," Satterfield offered, glancing at the aces in his hand and pushing a dollar into the pot. "I'm gonna raise you greenhorns fifty cents."

"You're about to lose a half-day's wages," Cook grinned,

meeting the raise. Then he said, "Wouldn't be a hunting party, not this time of year."

"Not less'n they're hunting steers," Satterfield added.

"We better check it out tomorrow," said Seltry. "Maybe Junior can send Davis and Wellman up thataway to look around. We got more'n we can do to sweep them cows back this way in time for the brandin'."

"Looks like Mr. Garfield's gonna have hisself a lotta steers to sell," Satterfield said, raking in the pot. "We've come up with a lot of unbranded stuff."

"Well, he'll like that," said Junior Wayburn, stepping into the bunkhouse. "We're holdin' a right good herd on the south range now. Soon's we get 'em separated an' culled we're gonna throw 'em in with herds from the Tumbler, the Willets, an' the Rockin' R and drive 'em to Roswell. May come up with two, three thousand head for sale, all the ranches combined."

"What's goin' on, anyway?" Satterfield asked. "This's too late for a spring roundup and a lot too early for the fall."

"Man in Roswell got a government contract he's got to fill now," Junior said. "He come to us, and Garfield and the others agreed to send him the cows."

"Well, that's good for Garfield," Satterfield said.

"Better break it up, boys," Junior ordered. "Hard day tomorrow, an' old Rooster over there'll start crowing before long."

By the clock on the mantle over the open fireplace, it was ten o'clock.

All hands turned in.

Quay wondered about those riders in the hills, wondering if they were the same who had taken Robert Murphy's life. He also thought about the exchange of looks by Arapaho Joe and Spider Wellman when Seltry mentioned the riders. What did that mean? He went to sleep with questions running through his mind.

Partial darkness still shrouded the windows of the Lazy G bunkhouse when Quay was awakened by a crowing rooster.

"Shut that thing up," Benny Satterfield shouted, and a moment later, in the dim light filtering through the windows, Quay saw a boot fly through the air and land with a thud near the end bunk. Peering closer, he saw Rooster Red standing on his knees in his bunk, head tilted upward, eyes bulging, crowing loudly.

"Where's my gun?" Hook Nelson asked, rolling out of bed. "We'll have fried chicken for dinner."

Someone lighted the lamp and the cowboys all came up, pulling on clothing and stamping their feet into boots. Quay noted the peculiarity of the way these men dressed. Each put his hat on first, then his pants. Boots came next, and after that, shirts. Some donned vests, and all wrapped gunbelts around their waists or hips.

Junior stepped over to Quay's bunk, buttoning his shirt. "The johnny's out back," he said, "an' you can foller the other boys to the washstand. Breakfast'll be ready as soon as you are, I reckon."

Later, after several eggs and a slab of beef, with cathead biscuits and thick, black coffee, Quay saddled his horse and led him from the corral. Junior was there, watching. The other hands had departed for chores.

"I'm obliged to you," Quay said. "You've fed me well and given me a place to sleep."

"Any time," Junior laughed. "The latch is up anytime you come this way."

"I've never spent this much time on a ranch before," Quay said. "It's strange to me."

"S'pect so," Junior returned. "Come back and I might give you a job so's you can get a real taste of ranchin'. We'll be a couple hands short in a week or two, I guess."

"Why so?"

"Took on a couple of temporary men to help with this roundup. They'll be leaving when we're through."

"Arapaho Joe and Spider Wellman," Quay said, not making it a question.

"That's the two," Junior said. "How'd you know?"

Quay thought better about saying anything about the suspicions they had aroused in him the night before. He said, "Oh, they just seemed to be apart from the other hands."

"That's pretty observant."

"Something else I wanted to ask you," Quay said. "How far can I trust Deputy Frazier?"

"Oh, all the way, I think," Junior said. "He's honest enough — just lazy. He'd like to draw his pay without gettin' up in the morning. But he'll steer you straight, especially if it seems to him you're doing what he ought to be doing."

"I'm not sure I know what I am doing," Quay confided. "I think I'm going in circles. When I went to sleep last night I was thinking that I'm not getting any answers, but I keep getting plenty of questions."

"The more questions you raise, the more likely you'll be to get some of 'em answered," the foreman said. "But there's one thing I'd advise you to do. You better start packin' iron."

"What's that?"

"A gun. Carry a gun. You're getting deeper in this thing all the time. You've got me believing that the deaths of Titlow and your friend are tied together somehow. You ask any more questions and somebody may come looking for you."

"I've got a gun in my saddlebags," Quay said, "but I'm not sure I could use it."

"You afraid?"

"No, not that. I've never used a gun."

"Have you fired a rifle?"

"Yes, I can shoot a rifle."

"Then get a rifle and carry it wherever you go. You can't afford to be unarmed anymore." He thought a moment and added, "And don't be afraid to use the rifle. There're times out here when you've got a split-second to make up your mind. Sometimes you'll have to shoot first and ask questions later."

Quay stepped up in the saddle, touched his hat to Junior, and trotted his horse out of the ranch yard. The horse wanted exercise this morning, and Quay let him have his head. He trotted briskly down the road and was still at a trot when they intersected the road to Reynaldo.

On the road coming from his left and also heading toward Reynaldo, were two riders, moving at a good gait. Quay sat his horse a moment, thinking there was something familiar about the two, and he was about to move on when he recognized Pearl and Zeb Willet. He reined back and waited for them to catch up.

"Good morning," he said, and both returned his greeting. Pearl wore a broad smile, as if she were happy to see him again. "If you're going to town, may I ride in with you?"

"Please do," Pearl said. Zeb spurred his horse ahead so the two could converse without his interference. Pearl rode side-saddle, her long skirt flowing back to the horse's flank. Quay was again taken with her beauty; he had never seen a girl quite as lovely. Her hair was pulled back in a bun, and she wore a hat perched on the front of her head.

"We're going for supplies," Pearl said. "Father didn't want me to come alone; so Zeb is escorting me. If I'd known we would meet you, he could have stayed home."

They chatted pleasantly for a few minutes, and she asked, "What brings you out our way again?"

"Actually," he confessed, "I haven't been back to town since I was at your place. I spent that night in the hills, enjoying the scenery, and last night I stayed at the Lazy G."

"How is Mr. Garfield?"

"He wasn't there. But if he had been, he would have been busy. They're rounding up cattle for a buyer in Roswell."

"Yes, so are we," she said. "That's why we need to be home instead of going to town. Each of the four ranches on this side of the basin is putting five hundred head into the herd."

"That's a lot of work for the three at your place."

"The four," she said, eyes flashing. "I've been helping. I rode all day yesterday, chasing cattle out of the brush."

"But why didn't your father hire more hands?"

"Oh, there were two who came to us and asked for jobs, but Father didn't like their looks and told them to leave. Zeb had to come and help him before he could get rid of them."

"When was that?"

"Late last week. Father thought they were too rough-looking."

Quay thought of Arapaho Joe and Spider Wellman at the Lazy G, but held his tongue about them.

"What did these men look like?" Quay asked.

"One was an Indian," she said. "An Apache, I think. He had a band around his head, holding back his hair, and he was short and stout — and ugly." She thought a moment about that and corrected herself: "Not ugly, exactly. Mean. Cruel. He had very cruel features."

He filed that information in his mind. Interesting, he thought.

"Do you mind if I ask you a question, Mr. Quay?" she asked.

"Only if you never call me Mr. Quay again," he laughed.

"All right. What should I call you? John?"

"Yes. Or Quay. Most people call me that."

"Are you making any headway in your investigation of Robert's death?"

He thought about that for a moment, then replied, "I honestly don't know. I'm slowly uncovering bits of information, but none of it fits together. Not yet, anyway."

"You sound as if you expect it to."

"I'm certainly hoping it does. I'd hate to think someone could do what was done to Robert and get away scot-free."

They reached town by mid-morning and rode in on Reynaldo's main street. An old dog raised himself from his morning snooze and looked at the three as they rode by. Chickens pecked in the street in front of the hardware and feed store. A half-dozen folks were on the street and a ranch wagon stood in front of the general store, the horses harnessed to it standing hip-shot in the warming sun. A few horses were tied to hitch rails up and down the street. Reynaldo was quiet this morning.

Before they parted, Quay asked, "Do you know where Mrs. Titlow lives? The stage manager's widow."

"Yes. Their house is just behind the station. You can't miss it. It's the only one there."

He thanked her, said how much he enjoyed riding with her, and turned his horse away.

Riding to the head of Main Street, he circled the stage station. An unhitched stage stood outside on the street, and a hostler was just bringing the teams out to hitch up when Quay rode around the place. He spotted the house immediately, a small, white-painted cottage surrounded by a whitewashed picket fence. The place was spotless and flowers grew in profusion in the yard.

Tying his horse to the fence, he opened the gate, which he noticed did not squeak, and walked up to the porch, knocking on the door. Inside, he heard soft footsteps approaching, and the door was opened by a woman of sixty, her gray hair tied behind her head. She was small, and Quay thought she had been at one time a very beautiful woman.

"Good morning, young man," she said.

"Are you Mrs. Titlow?" he asked, and when she nodded he said, "My name is John Quay. I am a friend of the young man who was murdered out on the range a few days ago."

She pushed open the screen door. "Please come in, Mr.

Quay. I was a friend of the other man who was murdered that day." She chuckled at the way she phrased that, and said, "I am Irene Titlow."

He stepped inside the door. The interior of the house was bright and sunny and immaculately clean.

"Please have a chair," she indicated a small rocking chair, and he sat in it.

"Mrs. Titlow, I'm trying to get information on my friend's death, and, I suppose, on the death of your husband, too. I can't help but feel they were connected."

"I have wondered about that, too," she said. "What information can I give you?"

"I'm not sure," he said. "I seem to be running in circles, gathering information in bits, but nothing fits together yet. Your husband was the station manager, wasn't he?"

"He was. We had been here almost twenty years. We loved it, both the town and the people. It has been a nice, quiet place to live until these last two weeks."

"Yes, ma'am. What did your husband do at the station?"

"He was manager, like I said."

"I mean, could you tell me what his duties were? In detail, please. We might discover something there."

"Of course. He did not do the outside work any longer because of his health. He had a hostler and a stable lad. Mostly what he did was the lighter work inside. The hostler and stable boy delivered any freight that came in. Mr. Titlow sold the tickets, made out shipping orders, and handled the mail, both incoming and outgoing. He usually delivered the mail downtown personally. He also kept the company books. He was quite busy."

"Yes, I can imagine he was."

"May I offer you some tea?" she asked. "It won't take a moment to fix."

"Yes, thanks, that would be nice," he said, and while she was away, he looked around the room. A tintype of a bald man of about sixty rested on a table. He assumed it was of her husband. The house was well furnished and appeared to be comfortable. He thought the Titlows had lived good lives in Reynaldo.

She returned in a few minutes with a small tray of cups and saucers and a teapot and cookies. Graciously, she poured, and he enjoyed the delicacy of her movements. She was quite the lady.

"Mrs. Titlow, what time was your husband killed?"

"At about three in the afternoon, I think. I was told of his death about four o'clock."

"Did you see anyone in the office with him?"

"Goodness, no," she said. "I never bothered going to the office. I didn't want to appear to be interferring with Mr. Titlow's business. I only went there in emergencies."

"Then you saw no one approach the office?"

"No, no. No one."

"What about the hostler or the stable boy?"

"No. They were working in the barn."

"Did he have any other stages out that afternoon?"

"No. The last one had been gone about two hours. The southbound stage comes in the morning, and the northbound in early afternoon."

"Can you think of any reason someone would kill your husband? Had he had words with anyone? Had he perhaps recognized an old enemy on the stage? Or. . . ."

"Mr. Quay, Mr. Titlow had no enemies. He had never had enemies. And, no, I cannot think of even a remote reason why anyone would wish to harm Mr. Titlow."

"Mrs. Titlow, was anything missing from the station after your husband's death?"

"We haven't missed anything. If anything is gone, it was something that came in on the stage that day."

He stood and prepared to leave. She brought him his hat. "Oh, Mrs. Titlow, one thing more: Do you know if your husband knew my friend?"

"My goodness, yes," she said. "Mr. Titlow spoke of him often. He said your friend was a Yale man. Your friend received his mail at the station, and my husband knew him from that. They conversed quite a lot. You see, Mr. Titlow was from New Jersey, and he liked to talk to anyone who lived back that way."

Irene Titlow showed him to the door, thanked him for coming, and waved to him when he boarded his horse and turned away from the picket fence.

He had learned nothing of importance there, Quay thought. That Titlow and Robert were friends, or acquaintances, proved nothing. Titlow apparently knew everyone in town. . . in this part of New Mexico, in fact. There was nothing about Titlow's duties at the station that would give rise to suspicion.

Quay rode back down the main street of Reynaldo, and found himself glancing from beneath his wide hat brim, hoping to catch a glimpse of Pearl Willet, but she was not in sight.

He saw Deputy Frazier standing on the boardwalk and reined over.

"Nice day," the deputy said, and Quay was certain Frazier had forgotten his name again.

"I want to talk to you," Quay said, dismounting and tying his reins to the hitch rail. They walked inside.

"Well, what have you found out?" the deputy asked. "Anything I ought to know?"

"I have a lot more questions than I did before, but not many answers," Quay said. "I'm picking up bits of information here and there that may come together sometime. I don't know. What I need to know now is who was seen at the stage station the afternoon Titlow was killed."

"Titlow? What about Titlow? Do you think Titlow had something to do with your friend's death?"

"I don't know, but it seems to be too much of a coincidence that two men would be murdered on the same day in a place as small as this if their deaths didn't have something to do with one another. How long had it been since you'd had a cold-blooded murder here?"

"Oh, these cowhands go at each other about every Saturday night."

"Yes, but murder?"

"Mel Wayburn shot and killed Ben Wheeling not two months ago."

"Was it murder," Quay asked, "or a fair fight?"

"Reckon it was fair," the deputy answered. "All the boys said so. We never did nothin' about it. Then there was the time Rooster Red got shot. . . ."

"I'm talking about murder!" Quay snapped.

"I see your point."

"Then answer my question. Who was seen at the station that afternoon?"

"Well, two or three of the townfolks went up there for one reason or another," Frazier said, "and then there was an Indian."

"What Indian? Tell me about him."

"I didn't see him, but a couple of fellers did. Said he was Apache — least he looked Apache. He rode up about three in the afternoon and went in to the station. Nobody saw him leave, but his horse was gone, and so was he, when they found Titlow dead."

"Did anyone know the Indian?"

"Nobody had ever seen him before, to my knowledge."

"Has anyone seen him since?"

"Not as I know."

"An Apache came to the Willet place looking for work a few days ago," Quay said.

"You don't say? Did they hire him?"

"No."

"Hmmm."

Briefly, Quay filled in the deputy on the things he had learned, but Frazier could no more make heads or tails of them than Quay could. He said as much.

Quay told Frazier of Junior Wayburn's advice to start carrying a rifle. "Where can I get a rifle?" he asked. "I won't carry that pistol."

"I got one back here I'll give you," Frazier said. "Took it off a man a month or two ago and he's done left the country. It's a Winchester in right good shape. All you'll have to do is buy a box of shells. You can get 'em at the hardware across the street, or at the gun shop on down on this side."

Quay worked the action of the Winchester and was satisfied.

"Thanks," he said. "I'll check in every few days and we can bring each other up to date."

"Do that," Frazier said, "and while you're at it, boy, be careful. Don't want something to happen to you, like it did to your friend."

Stepping into the street, Quay came face to face with Pearl Willet. "Hello, again," she said, beaming, and then she looked questioningly at the rifle.

"Hello, Pearl," he said, and brandishing the rifle, laughed. "I must not be too popular. Everybody wants me to start carrying a gun."

"Please be careful," she said, earnestly.

"I will," he assured her. "Are you finished? Are you going back now?"

"I have to stop at the dressmaker's for about a half-hour," she said. "Then we'll go back. We bought so much Zeb can't get it on his horse. He's over at the livery renting a rig right now."

She started to turn away, then appeared to have an afterthought. "Why don't you come out for supper tonight?" she asked. "I'm going to make a peach cobbler."

"Well, I. . . ."

"You could even spend the night," she suggested. "We have a spare room — the one Robert stayed in."

"Then I'll be there about six," he said.

"Oh, good." She hurried down the street and he watched until she turned into the dressmakers, liking the way she looked and the way she moved.

A clatter of hooves on the hard-packed street brought his attention to two riders loping into town. They pulled up before the cantina, swung down, and tied their horses beside two others. Quay recognized Arapaho Joe Davis and Spider Wellman as they went into the cantina.

Puzzled, he walked across to the cantina and went inside. Davis and Wellman stood at the bar drinking and talking with a stranger. He started to duck back out but Wellman turned and saw him. Taking a deep breath he walked up to the three.

"Howdy," he said, and almost laughed at himself for adopting the Western greeting. "What brings you boys to town? I thought you'd be heading for Coldwater Canyon today to check out those tracks."

No one returned his greeting, but the bartender caught Quay's eye and shook his head slightly, then dropped his eyes to the glasses he was polishing.

"What we're doin' in town," Wellman said slowly, "ain't none of your business."

"Just trying to make conversation," Quay said. "Can I buy you a drink?"

"We got a drink."

"Sorry," Quay began, "I. . . ."

"Are you spyin' on us?"

"Of course not."

No one in the bar saw the imperceptible nod directed toward Wellman by the stranger with whom he and Davis had been talking.

"You tenderfoot whelp!" Wellman cried, and stepping away from the bar he swung a vicious right to Quay's jaw. The blow knocked Quay backward onto the dirt floor. Quickly, Junior Wayburn's words flashed through Quay's mind, "Shoot first and ask questions later," but just as quickly he discarded the rifle, leaped to his feet, and dove at Wellman.

They were about the same size, and Quay's rush hammered Wellman to the floor. Quay swung a right and landed it on Wellman's nose. Blood spurted, and before he could swing again, the blast of a shotgun startled him to a halt.

Leaning on the bar, the bartender covered the two with a double-barreled shotgun. "Outside, you two," he hissed. "I got one more bar'l an' I'll use it on the one who swings next in here." The sawdust on the dirt floor smoldered where the buckshot had struck.

Quay came to his feet, yanked Wellman off the floor by his shirt front, and propelled him through the swinging doors. He went after him in a rush, anger flooding through him. The saloon emptied and when Arapaho Joe and the stranger came through the door their hands were on their guns, but they skidded to a halt, looking into the barrel of a forty-five held unwaveringly in the hand of Zeb Willet.

"Let *them* fight it out," Zeb said.

Wellman lay in the street, and when Quay lunged for him he reached for the pistol at his side. A shot rang out from the street and Quay stopped again, watching Wellman's gunhand gripping his still-holstered six-gun. Curly Ford, Gus Braswell, and Sheep Calahan sat their horses in the street, Ford's forty-five smoking in his hand.

"Get rid of the gun, friend," Curly called to Wellman. "The other gent ain't armed, an' this's gonna be a fair fight."

Scowling, Wellman flipped the gun aside and ripped a right hand to Quay's midriff but it was a glancing blow as Quay twisted his body away and hammered Wellman with a left and right. He called on all the boxing skill he had learned at Yale and when Wellman rushed him he stepped aside. Wellman came back swinging and Quay parried his blows. Quay hooked a left that struck Wellman in the throat and made him gasp. Wellman countered with a left and right and drew blood from Quay's eyebrow.

Quay tied up Wellman's arms with a bear hug and wrestled him to the dirt, striking wickedly at the man's face. The blows brought blood.

Both men came to their feet and stood toe to toe, swinging. Quay parried most of Wellman's haymakers, landing short, telling punches that rocked Wellman's head. Then Quay stepped inside and hammered Wellman to the body and Wellman gave ground. He lunged for the pistol in the dirt and Quay beat him to it, kicking it into the gathering crowd.

Glancing around, Quay saw Pearl Willet among the spectators, and startled at her presence, dropped his guard and Wellman knocked him flat in the dirt. Momentarily stunned, his arms sprawled out, Quay met Wellman's rush with his feet, carrying Wellman over his head into a hitch rail with tremendous force.

Quay was on top of him in a flash. He jerked Wellman to his feet, turned him around, and planted a long shot on the side of his jaw. Wellman went down and as Quay reached for him, someone grabbed Quay from behind.

"That's enough," Sheep Calahan said, clutching Quay. "He's had it! You've beat him."

"Don't beat him to death," Quay heard Gus Braswell say, laughing.

Breathing heavily, Quay stepped away, then looked back at Wellman. The man was coming around, blood streaming down his face and splattering on his shirt, his jaw hanging at an odd angle. Arapaho Joe stared icily at Quay, his eyes spelling murder.

The stranger who had been with Davis and Wellman paid little attention to Quay. His dark, brooding eyes were on Pearl, and in them was written hunger. Zeb Willet noticed and stepped to his sister's side, his rifle barrel steady and directed toward the stranger.

The man pulled his gaze away from Pearl and stared icily at Zeb for a moment, then he joined Arapaho Joe and moved quickly to help Wellman to his feet and back into the cantina. Zeb covered them until they were inside, then followed through the door. In a moment he returned, saying, "Pearl, get him," he gestured to Quay, "and both of you get down the street away from here."

Pearl took Quay by the arm and the three hands from the Rocking R crowded around him.

"Please," she said, "let's get him away."

Zeb kept an eye on the cantina until Quay was ushered away, then he followed.

"Get Dr. Limbert," Pearl said, and Quay hushed her.

"I don't need the doc," he said. "I'm all right. It's just a little blood."

"Washstand behind the cafe here," Gus pulled Quay toward a narrow alley, and at the rear of the building Pearl washed the blood from Quay's face.

She daubed at the cut in his eyebrow with a handkerchief, and said, "You ought to let Dr. Limbert sew that up," but Quay felt the cut and laughed. "It's all right, Pearl. It's just a scratch."

She laughed, too.

"Wow!" she said. "You can fight!" She showed no skittishness in her appraisal, and Quay thought she must be accustomed to men fighting.

Everybody laughed, and Quay felt the anger go out of him. The tension eased. He brushed the dust from his clothes.

"Zeb," Curly asked, "did you see the way that ranny looked at Pearl?"

"I saw," Zeb said.

"Better find out who he is," Curly advised. "He'll be trouble for Pearl."

"May have to kill him," Zeb said, and there was no nonsense in his voice. Quay thought Zeb was not boasting but stating a fact as he saw it.

They chatted for a while in the street and when Zeb and Pearl broke away to go home, the Rocking R men took Quay to the Rimrock Saloon.

"Welcome, welcome," the bartender was short, bald, and paunchy. He wiped his hands on his white apron as the four came in the door. "Step up, gentlemen, drinks are on me. I saw the fight and congratulate the winner."

He put a bottle on the bar and Quay frowned.

"How about a sarsaparilla for our friend?" Curly grinned, and the bartender filled a glass and shoved it to him.

"There you are, and it's cold," he said, beaming. "My name's Grayson. These fellows know me, but I ain't met you."

Grinning broadly, Quay shook the bartender's hand. "John Quay here," he said. "Late of Yale College."

"You don't fight like a college man," Grayson said. "You fight like a saloon brawler."

"No, he don't," Braswell shouted. "Didn't you see him blockin' them punches? He fights like one of them boxers."

Curly said, "How about some victuals, Grayson? We'll be over there." The four took their drinks to a table.

"What brought that fight on?" Curly asked. "And who was the hombre you beat up?"

"I don't really know what started it," Quay said. "The man was Spider Wellman. The one Zeb covered was Arapaho Joe Davis, and I don't know the one they were with, the one Zeb said he may have to kill."

"Arapaho Joe Davis!" Curly whistled. "I know of him. He's supposed to be hell on wheels with a six-gun. And mean as a snake."

"They're helping the Lazy G with its roundup," Quay said, and Curly lifted his eyebrows.

"Wonder why Junior's hiring such as them?" Sheep asked.

"He said they showed up at the right time and he took them on to put the herd together," Quay answered.

"He must not know Arapaho Joe. He's a shorthorn killer from Texas," Sheep said.

"How do you know all this?" Curly asked Quay.

"I spent the night out there last night," Quay explained. "They're working hard, and when I saw Wellman and Davis go in the cantina, I wondered why they weren't working; so I went in to see if I could find out, and found them talking to that stranger."

"That stranger," the bartender said, hovering over the table, "is Rattler Baines. Anybody thinks Arapaho Joe Davis is ornery ain't met Rattler Baines. He's killed about as many men as you could count. Got a streak up his back a yard and a half wide, and it ain't yellow. It's white. He's pure skunk — but he's the fastest man alive with a gun. That's why they call him Rattler. He's quicker'n a rattlesnake an' twict as mean."

Braswell whistled. "Rattler Baines, huh? Quay, you're lucky Zeb Willet got the drop on him when they come out that cantina door, else we might be fitting you for a box along about now."

"Yeah," Quay said, "I know Zeb covered them, and I'm

going to shake his hand when I see him tonight."

"Tonight?"

"Pearl asked me to supper."

"Oh, ho," Curly grinned. "Are you gettin' sweet on her?"

"I could," Quay answered honestly. "You boys were right. She's surely a cooker and a looker, all rolled into one."

Grayson came to the table with a stack of *tortillas*, a huge bowl of *frijoles*, and four plates of eggs generously scrambled with onions and peppers.

"Wrap yourself around some of this," Curly said, grabbing the *frijole* bowl. "Eat a good bait of this stuff and you might be able to tackle Rattler Baines."

"Why'd you fight Wellman?" Sheep wanted to know, digging into the eggs and sighing at their taste. "Man, this is livin'!"

"When I asked what they were doing in town," Quay said, "he swung at me." He rubbed his chin. "Knocked me down. Hey," a thought came to him, "my rifle's still over there."

"Don't sweat it," Curly said. "It's right here. Zeb got it when he went back in and give it to me." He slid the Winchester over to Quay. "Take my advice, friend, an' don't get caught without this rifle. You're in this thing up to your ears. What have you learned so far?"

The food made Quay realize how hungry he was. He forked some of the eggs into his mouth, then speared a piece of pepper and shoved it in, and when he bit into the pepper he rose in his chair, trying to catch his breath, fanning at his mouth. Only a great draught of sarsaparilla saved him from burning to death, he thought, and it was minutes after he got his breath and wiped his eyes that he was able to talk again. He tried the *frijoles* and found them delectable, though a bit on the hot side, too.

Still wiping his eyes, he brought the trio up to date on what he had learned. Then he asked, "Have you hired any new hands on the Rocking R?"

"Yeah," Curly mused. "We took on two last week. Fernandez put 'em on for the roundup."

"They'd bear watching," Quay said, matter of factly. "Who are they?"

"Couple of local boys," Curly said. "Least, they've been around here for a while. Used to work for the Sixty-Eight. Names of Fairly and Johnson. Seem harmless, an' they're hard workers."

"They've done nothing to arouse suspicions?" Quay asked.

"Not in me," Curly said, and the other two agreed.

"By the way," Curly asked, "you said you went to the Lazy G lookin' for your friend's horse?"

"That's right."

"What kinda horse was it?"

"It was a big blue roan with four white stockings and a white dagger blazed on its face," Quay said.

"Strange," Curly said, "we saw one like that at the livery when we rode in."

"The livery here?" Quay asked.

"Right down the street," Curly said. "In the corral. Big, beautiful horse."

They bought a round and finished it, and Quay stood. "I'm going to see that horse."

"We'll go with you," Curly said, rising. Thanking Grayson, they walked out into the sunshine. Deputy Frazier stood on the boardwalk. He looked at the lumps, cuts, and assorted scratches on Quay's face.

"Welcome to the West," he said.

"You orta see the other fellow," Curly chided.

"Understand they took him to the doc," Frazier said. "I believe they said you like to broke his jaw, Mr. Quay."

Quay smiled. "At least it helped you remember my name."

"I ain't likely to forget it again," the deputy returned.

"We're on our way to the livery," Curly said, "to see a man about a horse."

"What horse?"

"Big blue roan, four white stockings, white blaze on its face."

"Maybe I better come along," Deputy Frazier said. The four mounted their horses and rode slowly toward the livery, the deputy walking beside them.

Quay saw the horse in the corral before they reached the stable. What a magnificent animal! Sleek and powerful and taller than any other horse Quay had seen since arriving in New Mexico, the horse raised his head and nickered at the approaching riders.

"He's beautiful!" Quay said, almost to himself.

"Never saw a prettier one," Curly laughed. "Nor a stouter one. He could go for days."

The hostler stepped out of the barn, pulling a thick

sheepskin coat together at his throat.

"Howdy, boys," he said. "What'cha reckon I can do for you?"

"Quay," Curly said, "this here is Eskimo Jack. Says he lived so long with the Eskimos he ain't been warm since."

Quay almost laughed, but saw Eskimo Jack was serious. "Pretty day," he said, "if it wasn't so cold." Quay looked out at the rangeland surrounding the town and in every direction saw heat waves rising.

"We want to talk to you about that horse," Frazier said, indicating the blue roan.

"Him? Bought him off a feller this mornin'. Paid him twenty-five dollars hard cash."

"Twenty-five dollars for a hundred-dollar animal?" Frazier asked. "Didn't you suspect anything?"

"Nary a thing," Eskimo Jack returned. "Man wanted to sell, an' he was in a hurry."

"You got a bill of sale, I reckon?"

"Yessir, got it right here in m'pocket." He fished out a crumpled piece of paper.

"What's the name of the man sold the horse to you?"

"Didn't give no name," Eskimo Jack said, "but he signed the paper — right there."

Frazier took the bill of sale. "It's signed, all right. Signed by a dead man."

"Huh?" Eskimo Jack couldn't follow the trail the sheriff was on. "He was alive when he signed it."

Frazier handed the paper to Quay. "Is that your friend's signature?"

The bill, indeed, was signed by Robert Murphy, but the handwriting was strange. "No, it isn't," Quay said. "I have a letter from Robert Murphy in my saddlebags." He dismounted and went through the saddlebags until he found the letter. The signatures were different.

"What did the man look like sold you the horse?" Frazier asked.

"Little feller. Not as tall as me. Not as fat, neither. Didn't have no upper front teeth. Knocked out in a fight, I guess. Got one knocked out myself one time. Know how that feels."

"Cowhand?"

"Looked like it. Wore the garb."

"Ever seen him before?"

"No. First time I ever laid eyes on him."

"Where did he go when you paid him?"

"Straight to the saloon. Where else?"

"Which saloon?"

"The cantina down there."

"I reckon you bought a stolen horse," Frazier said.

Eskimo Jack snapped his head toward the sheriff. "I don't know nothin' about that. Feller offered me a deal, I paid him, an' he signed the bill of sale. That don't say the hoss was stoled."

"I say it was stolen," Frazier said. "This horse belonged to the young man who was killed last week."

"No skin off my nose. I didn't know nothin' about it bein' stoled."

"You didn't even wonder," Frazier asked slowly, "when the man said he'd take twenty-five dollars for a horse worth four times that much?"

"No, sir, I didn't wonder at all," he shivered and pulled the sheepskin tighter.

"I'm not sure a jury of stockmen would believe you."

"Jury? What'cha talkin' about, jury?"

"I may have to hold you for receiving stolen goods," Frazier said.

"Now, wait a minute, sheriff. I done tol' you I didn't know this hoss was stoled."

"Boys," the sheriff addressed the Rocking R hands, "would any of you recognize this horse's tracks?"

"I would," Braswell said. "The hoss the dead man rode had a nick out of its front left shoe. Big nick. Quarter of an inch wide."

"Jack," Frazier looked straight at the hostler, "if that front left shoe has a nick, I'm takin' you in, maybe as an accessory to murder."

"What's that?"

"That's helpin' kill somebody."

"I didn't hep kill nobody."

"Curly, raise that horse's front left hoof," Frazier ordered. "See if it's got a nick in the shoe."

"Wait a minute, Sheriff," Curly interjected, picking up on Frazier's intentions. "We can straighten this out. He can swap the horse to Quay here for his."

Eskimo Jack looked at Quay's horse. "Not for that nag, no, sir!"

"Then you'd better come with me," Frazier said.

"But. . . ." Quay started to protest but Curly silenced him with a hand on his arm.

BOB TERRELL

"I might take some boot," Eskimo Jack allowed.

"No boot. Even up, or you come with me."

"All right. Even up. Make me a bill of sale for your'n," he said to Quay, "an' don't sign no dead man's name on it."

"But I. . . ." Quay had another protest on his lips.

"Shut up an' sign," Curly said.

"You're tradin' the riggin', too," Frazier said.

"Oh, no, I ain't. His saddle ain't worth a plug nickel."

"Even up," Frazier said. "Horses and saddles, or I'll run you in. You've traded for stolen hosses before, Jack, and I looked the other way. But not this time. You make the trade or, by thunder, I'll lock you up and throw away the key."

"Dang it, Sheriff, a man's got a right to make a livin'."

"Not on stolen goods. Not in this town," Frazier replied, his anger rising, and Quay admired Frazier's sudden stiffening of backbone.

Quay found his own bill of sale and signed it. Eskimo Jack took it grudgingly.

"Thanks," Quay said.

"An' don't you come round here 'spectin' me to put up your hoss," Jack wailed.

Quay untied his saddlebags and tied them behind the saddle Curly had put on the roan. The saddle itself was worth more than Quay's entire outfit, horse and saddle together.

"Mount up, men," Frazier said. "Pleasure doin' business with you, Jack, but you better remember what I said about stolen goods."

Out of earshot, Quay could hold back no longer.

"Deputy," he said, "I didn't intend to steal this horse from him."

"You didn't steal it," Frazier replied. "He's got a twenty-five dollar horse and a ten-dollar saddle. He didn't lose no money, and it gives him more than he deserves, I'd say."

"But, this horse is worth four times more than mine. You said so yourself."

"So I did, and it is. But if you keep galavantin' around these parts, you may need a real horse under you. Put that rifle in the boot and let's look that horse over for wounds."

The five went over every part of the horse but found no wounds.

"Must not have hit the hoss," Gus said. "The blood we found where it fell must've come from the rider."

"Reckon you're right," Curly said. "This horse is sound

85

as a dollar."

Quay could not believe his good fortune. He walked around the horse, studying it. It was truly magnificent. It's eyes showed an intelligence few others portrayed.

"He'll get you there an' back," Frazier said, also eyeing the horse.

"His name's Dagger," Quay said, and melancholy almost overcame him. "I've got Robert's horse, but I'm no nearer solving his murder than when I started."

The other four remained silent; not one of them agreed.

No one in Reynaldo had to wait long for Rattler Baines to strike. He was a little man who carried a big gun, and he earned two more notches that afternoon.

Grafton Tumbler, owner of the Tumbleweed, the northernmost ranch of the four in line east of Reynaldo, rode into town in a carriage, accompanied by his foreman, Big John Radcliff. Tumbler went straight to the law office of Braxton Smith to transact business, and Radcliff set about purchasing supplies for the ranch.

They had been in town only about a half-hour when Baines rode up the street from the livery stable where he had quartered his horse overnight. He swung down at the Rimrock Saloon. Inside he ordered a drink at the bar and stood with one foot on the brass rail.

Two hands from the Hook-Eye southwest of Reynaldo sat at a table in a corner, talking in low tones, occasionally laughing, obviously enjoying an afternoon away from work.

They noticed that Rattler Baines appeared to be waiting for someone. He glanced often at the batwing doors, checked his pocket watch twice, and ordered another drink, which he took to a nearby table. He sat facing the door and began to sip his whiskey.

Wilson, the leatherworker, came in and ordered a beer. "Hot, ain't it?" Wilson said to Grayson, the proprietor.

"Hottest since last summer," Grayson returned. "Getting dry, too, out on the range. So they tell me."

The batwings swung again and Grafton Tumbler and Big John Radcliff came in. They went straight to the bar and ordered whiskey. Tumbler, a man of slight build and perhaps fifty years, took off his hat and wiped his brow.

The butt of a six-gun showed above his waistband. Radcliff, a giant of a man in range garb, wore a pistol in a holster at his waist, resting comfortably over his hip bone.

"Howdy, Mr. Tumbler," Wilson greeted. "I've got that harness you wanted almost finished. You can pick it up in a day or two."

"Thanks, Wilson," Tumbler smiled. "John here can send someone in for it. You just say when."

"Are you Grafton Tumbler?" a voice asked from behind the rancher, who turned to look into the dark, beady eyes of Rattler Baines, now on his feet behind the table he occupied.

"Yes, sir," Tumbler returned. "What can I do for you?"

"You can give me back the cows you rustled off my range," Baines's voice was flat and deadly. His lifted his hands over the butts of the twin forty-fives at his sides.

"I beg your pardon, sir," Tumbler said, his voice agitated, "but I have rustled no cows of yours, nor of anyone else's. What ranch are you from?"

"I represent the WXL."

"The WXL?" Tumbler furrowed his brow. "I'm not even familiar with your brand. Never saw it. You've got the wrong man."

"I've got the right one," Baines hissed, "and you're a liar. You've been rustling my stock for months."

"Sir, I resent. . ." Tumbler took a step toward Baines — his last step.

Baines shot him through the heart.

"Here!" Big John Radcliff roared, and went for his gun. Baines shot him with his other pistol, pulling it swiftly from the holster and placing the slug precisely to the left of Big John's shirt pocket.

Both men were dead when they hit the floor.

The Hook-Eye hands came to their feet, round eyes staring in disbelief. Behind the bar, Grayson stood paralyzed.

Rattler Baines shucked the empty shells from his revolvers and slowly and deliberately reloaded, shoved the weapons in his holsters, turned his back on the grisly scene, and walked out. A moment later Grayson heard the clatter of hooves outside.

Grayson recovered and shouted to the Hook-Eye hands, "Go get the sheriff. Be quick!"

One of the punchers ran out the door and almost collided with Deputy Frazier coming in. "What's going on in here?" Frazier's voice was loud in the silence of the saloon, and then he saw the crumpled bodies on the floor and immediately recognized Tumbler by his expensive suit and Radcliff by his bulk.

"Here! Here! Who did this?" Frazier wanted to know.

"Stranger to me," one of the punchers shook his head. "Never saw him before. Accused Mr. Tumbler of rustling his stock and when Tumbler objected, he shot him dead. Then he pulled his other gun and shot Radcliff."

"It was Rattler Baines," said a voice behind him, and Frazier turned to see Grayson, the bartender. "I've seen him before."

Others came into the saloon to see what the shooting was about, and Frazier asked the Hook-Eye men, "Did you both see it?"

"Saw it," said the one who had almost collided with Frazier in the door. "Have to call it a fair fight — if a fight with Rattler Baines can be fair. Both of these men were armed, and Tumbler took a step toward Baines. When Baines killed Tumbler, this other gent went for his gun and Baines pulled out his second iron and shot him dead."

Frazier looked at the other Hook-Eye hand, who said, "Yep, it was fair enough. But Baines goaded them into it."

Frazier looked at Grayson.

"I have to agree with these boys," Grayson said. "It was fair, I reckon, but Mr. Tumbler wasn't a rustler. Baines picked a fight. He was in here a half-hour or more, waiting for them."

"How do you know he was waiting for them?"

"He kept looking at his watch and at the door, and when they came in, he stood up right over there and began to bait them, accusing them of rustling."

"But the fight was fair, you say?"

"Yes, I'd have to say that."

"Somebody get Doc Limbert," Frazier said. "He'll take care of the bodies. Need a man to ride out to the Tumbleweed and tell Mrs. Tumbler."

Two men left the saloon, and a few minutes later Dr. Limbert came in with a small black satchel. He removed a stethoscope, listened to each man's chest, and shook his head. "Dead, all right," he said. "I'll need some help to get them over to my place." He had plenty of volunteers.

Quay had been sleeping soundly in the hotel since early

afternoon. He rose at four, bathed, and dressed in fresh clothing. Buttoning his shirt, he looked out the window onto Main Street and saw several knots of people standing on the boardwalk talking in hushed tones. Frowning, he quickly finished dressing, took up his rifle, and went downstairs. On the boardwalk, Frazier stood talking to a crowd that included Curly, Gus, and Sheep, and others. Quay walked up.

"What's going on?" he asked.

"Where you been?" Frazier asked.

"In my room asleep."

"You must sleep pretty sound," Frazier said. "Two men gunned down three doors away and you didn't hear a thing."

"Gunned down? Who?"

"Tumbler and his foreman," Curly answered. "Rattler Baines shot 'em."

Quay got the details quickly and looked quizically at the deputy.

"Fair fight," Frazier said defensively. "Can't do a thing."

Frazier told the story of the fight as it had been told to him. When he mentioned the WXL brand he said, "Nobody ever heard of the WXL. Might be over the Texas line somewhere."

"In that dry land?" Sheep said. "Not likely. Any ranch over there would have to be big enough to be known."

A Sixty-Eight puncher joined in. "The WXL? I've seen that brand. Bunch of punchers drove a WXL herd into Fort Sumner a year or so ago. Five hundred head or thereabouts. But they said it was a road brand. They bought some stock, road branded it, and drove the herd to Sumner to sell to the army."

He dug back in his memory, trying to recapture details. "Come to think of it," he said, brightening, "Rattler Baines was with that crowd."

"Are you shore?" Frazier asked.

"Yeah, you don't forget seein' Rattler Baines," the puncher avowed. "It was him, all right."

"I'd better telegraph the sheriff," Frazier said, and as he started to leave, a rider galloped up the street, making more haste than one should in town, except in an emergency.

Frazier shaded his eyes. "It's Old Man Willet," he said. "He's in a hurry."

Willet saw Frazier on the boardwalk and hailed him.

Tying to the hitch rail, he said, "Got something you oughta see, Frazier," but all had already noticed the fresh cowhide tied behind his saddle.

He spread out the hide and it was clearly branded with a WXL.

"Well, I'll be!" Frazier ejaculated. "First one I ever saw."

"That ain't all," Willet said and flipped the cowhide over. On the inside, only the "W" showed as old scar tissue. The "XL" wound was fresh.

"Cuss me if somebody ain't branded one of your steers, Willet."

"Not just one," Willet said. "The boys found a pocket of 'em up in the hills, an' ever' steer they brought in wore the WXL. We knowed they was our steers because an old mossyhorn we all knew was in the bunch. We skinned this one out and there 'tis."

"Somebody's been using a runnin' iron," the deputy said.

"No, they ain't," Willet disagreed. "They've got a fixed brand. We skinned out another steer and it's brand is exactly the same as this one. Ain't a man here could make two identical brands with a runnin' iron. They forged the iron to fit exactly over my W."

"He's right," Curly agreed. "It'd take an artist to do it otherwise."

R attler Baines rode out of town to the south, chuckling over the shock registered on the faces of Grafton Tumbler and Big John Radcliff when he went for his gun. "Both of 'em saw what was comin'," he said to his horse, and laughed aloud. "That ought to occupy everybody's mind for a while. Take their minds off other things — " he laughed again "— like losin' a few steers."

Ice water flowed through the veins of Rattler Baines, and the last vestige of human decency had been stripped from him long ago.

He rode a desert grulla, a wiry little horse that wouldn't win any races but would still be plugging along when the thoroughbreds had fallen with fatigue.

Rattler's black, flat-crowned hat accentuated the leanness of his deeply-tanned face. A wisp of a mustache lined his upper lip, and his eyes, unlike those of most killers of the West, were dark, almost obsidian. He was a small man, making him a poorer target, he always joked, but there was nothing small about the twin forty-fives he wore on his hips. Pound for pound, he was probably the most dangerous man in the West because he had a profound lack of scruples. Even in the most dreaded Western killers, though, there sometimes ran a streak of decency that surfaced at times. Not with Rattler Baines. There seemed to be little about him that was human. He cared nothing for anyone else, not even those with whom he worked, and he seldom associated with any of them. Only when there was a killing to be done, or a job to be handled, did he break down and ride with others. He was a loner, and he especially detested the Apache with whom he was often forced to team.

The barbaric ways of the Apache did not bother him; he simply didn't like the man. But he respected him and often walked a little wider around the Indian to keep from antagonizing him. No need in having to kill a man as good with a knife as the Apache. Such skill often came in handy in their line of work.

Rattler and his brother Sam came out of central Texas soon after the War Between the States. For a while, they helped push cattle up the trail to the Kansas markets. Sam was handy with pots and pans and victuals and became a cook of note among the drovers. Often, when drovers with other herds learned that Sam Baines was cooking for a particular herd, they found reason to visit that herd's campfire about suppertime. No one could refuse seconds on Sam's apple pie.

But Rattler had no interest in cooking, nor even in driving cattle up the trail. Granted, it was a cattle drive that got him out of the poverty of reconstruction Texas, and when he reached Kansas where money flowed more freely, he decided to stay. His father was a Methodist preacher of sorts in Fort Worth who tried to raise four sons after Rattler's mother died. With three, Rattler decided, the old man had done all right. One was a barber in Fort Worth, another a puncher for cattle ranches down along the Rio Grande. Sam was the third and he had become a good cook, albeit he had kept bad company all these years, and he, Rattler, was the fourth. Apparently he hadn't given his father much reason for pride during his growing-up years. His dad used to look at him and say, "They's one in ever' bar'l — and you're it in mine."

He laughed aloud. "That was some barrel, hoss," he said.

Robbing and killing and all the skills of banditry came easily for Baines where there was profit to be made, and when other unscrupulous men learned of his prowess with a gun, they often hired him to do their own dirty work, which he cherished because the paydays were good and the payoff always stood at the end of the action. He had always eaten higher on the hog than his daddy, the preacher, and thus he reconciled his deeds.

He became so skilled, so swift in putting himself into action with the two forty-fives he always wore, and so indiscriminate about his targets, that folks began to call him Rattler. The name stuck, and no one remembered his given name. Sometimes even Sam Baines had trouble remembering that Rattler Baines was christened Edward Sydney Baines. He became Rattler all over the West, and during the twenty years since the end of the war his reputation had grown to parallel that of the most notorious killers.

He was now forty-four, an age that few gunslingers attained. Jesse James was cut down at the age of thirty-five. Hickok made it to thirty-nine and Johnny Ringo to thirty-eight. He knew. He kept up with them. Ben Thompson and King Fisher were killed last year, Thompson at forty-one and Fisher at the tender age of thirty. William Bonney checked out at twenty-one, but he raised enough hell for three lifetimes in those short years.

"I've beat 'em all," he said, again addressing his horse. And then he turned philosophical for a moment: "Oh, well, live by the gun, die by the gun." He had forgotten who he had heard say that. "I'm gonna beat that. There ain't a one of 'em can beat old Rattler. I'm gonna live forever, hoss; if they can't beat me, who can?"

How many men had been killed by those who came to his mind as he rode down the desert road? Hundreds, he guessed. Wes Hardin had dispatched more than forty men before he went to prison at twenty-four in 1877. Shucks, Wes had been in jail for eight years now, building twenty-five years, but he had howled while loose.

Some killers carved notches in the handles of their weapons, one for every man killed by the gun. Jesse James drove tacks in the walnut grip of his pistol for the men he killed. Rattler thought that was showing off too much. He hadn't even kept track of the number he'd killed, no more than he had counted the women he'd had, but riding along with nothing else to occupy his mind he counted back over his long, bloody trail and came up with the number thirty-three, counting the two men he had just killed in Reynaldo. "An' that," he spoke to the horse again, "don't count Injuns and Mexicans."

He came to an intersecting track that led eastward. The road he traveled continued southward toward Roswell. Pulling up his horse, he sat in the intersection and contemplated which way to go, finally pulling his horse to the left to take the eastward trail. "This'll get us back to camp," he said, "an' maybe that's where we ought'a go."

Fifteen minutes of riding brought him to another fork in the trail. The right fork, he knew, went on into the mountains, and the left fork, he had previously determined, led back to the Willet Ranch and thence to the other ranches to the north.

"Hey," he pulled up his horse. "What say we take the trail to the Willet place? Might be we could get lucky with that filly there."

Touching the grulla with his spurs, he galloped up the road, coming shortly to the turnoff to the Willet spread, and fifty yards on the turnoff he rode through the gate that led on to the ranch. He observed that the gate served no purpose other than identifying the ranch. There were few fences in this section of New Mexico and likely to be none of major import until settlers began arriving to cut pieces off the free range and plow the ground away.

Pearl had finished her chores and sat on the porch, resting and waiting until she had to begin preparing dinner. She wanted to make some special dishes for Quay and she ran recipes through her mind.

She saw the rider top the hill to the west and come in under the sun, and thought perhaps it was Zeb or possibly her father. It was not Ray; that she could tell by the way he rode. Suddenly, she sat upright and shaded her eyes against the sun and stared long at the approaching rider. It was neither Zeb nor her father, but a stranger. He swung along aboard a grulla, bouncing more than her father or either of her brothers, all of whom were out on the range tending to the roundup of the five hundred steers they would soon ship to Roswell. Maybe it was Quay, arriving early, but he had never ridden a grulla and likely wouldn't if the livery had any other animal available.

Moving inside the house, she continued to look at the rider, and instinctively checked the rifle rack beside the door. Three Winchesters stood butts down in the rack. She picked up the nearest one and checked its loads. Fully loaded. She stood it back in the rack.

The rider now approached the ranch yard and when he rode in, the grulla kicking up dust from the yard, she recognized the man as Rattler Baines, and her heart suddenly came up in her throat as fright gripped her.

Calming herself, she stepped onto the porch as Baines dismounted and began to tie the grulla to the hitchrail.

"Mr. Baines," she said, making an effort to hold her voice steady, "if you wish to water your horse, the trough is over by the corral," she nodded in that direction and he looked

95

to see the trough. "You may have all the water you want, but if, by chance, you came for any other reason, I would strongly suggest that you mount up and leave immediately. You are not welcome here."

"Why, sister," Baines said, mirth playing through his eyes, "you ain't bein' a bit hospitable. Why'n't you ask me to come in an' eat? I'm hungry."

"I'm sorry," she said. "I have nothing for you to eat."

"Yes, you do, dearie," he said, rounding the hitch rail and reaching the steps to the porch. "You shorely do."

She stepped back into the house and Baines lunged up the steps and across the porch. He saw her running into the dining room and crossed the living room to the dining room door. She stood at the opposite end of the dining table, and he began to grin again. "You can't hide from me, miss; you may as well come on around the table and let's be friends for a while."

"My father and brothers will be home soon," she said. "You had better leave while you still can."

"Your father and brothers don't worry me," he said. "But they'd better worry you. If they come before I'm through here, they'll be dead men. I done killed two men today. . ." and he laughed as she caught her breath sharply, ". . .an' I reckon two or three more won't matter much."

"Please leave!" she shouted at him, but he bolted around the left side of the table. Instantly, she came around the other side, jerking chairs into the floor as she ran.

She dashed into the living room and toward the rifle rack as she heard him fall over the overturned chairs and clatter cursing to the floor.

When he righted himself and jumped into the living room, he looked into the barrel of a .30-caliber Winchester held steady in her feminine hands. The barrel of the gun did not waver, and he could see that the weapon was fully cocked and her finger was on the trigger.

"Now, take it easy, girlie," he said, slowly advancing toward her.

"I am taking it easy, Mr. Baines," she replied and her voice was steady, "but you take one more step and I'll shoot you in the brisket. If you don't think I can hit what I aim at, try me. You've only your life to lose."

He halted and reconnoitered the situation. Certain

that the girl could shoot, and would, indeed, shoot him in the brisket, he backed away, lowering his hands toward his hips.

Instantly, she brought the rifle barrel up until it pointed directly into his face. "Raise your hands immediately, Mr. Baines. If you come near your pistols, I shall shoot."

Believing her, he began edging for the door.

"I didn't mean you no harm, lady," he said. "I only come acallin', an' if I ain't welcome I'll just be on my way. But you've shore got a high-handed way of treating those who call on you."

"Those who call on me at my invitation receive much better treatment," she said, "but you will never know that because I do not ever want to see your face again." She advanced on him as he went out the door, moving quickly enough to keep him in sight.

"Girlie, you be careful how you handle that rifle," he said. "It might go off."

"If it goes off, Mr. Baines, it will kill you."

"Not you," he laughed. "Rattler Baines ain't gonna meet his end at the hands of no girl. It'll take some kind of a man to get rid of me."

"Please be assured that a girl can kill as easily and as deadly as a man," she said. "If you do not want to be killed by a girl, I would advise you to stay away from here. The next time I see you on Willet range, I will shoot. And Mr. Baines, when I shoot, I will shoot to kill."

He started to protest again, but she dropped the rifle barrel and pulled the trigger, and the slug kicked up dust an inch from his boot. He leaped into the air and when he came down he lunged for his saddle, mounting and wheeling the grulla.

As he pounded out of the yard, she heard him yell, "I'll be back, girlie. You can count on that."

She fired another round past his head and he hunched deeper into the grulla's mane, jabbing the horse with already-bloody spurs.

As he bounced back up the road, she sat in one of the porch chairs, still clutching the smoking rifle, and watched him until he became only a dot on the horizon. Then he was gone, and she realized she had been holding her breath. She exhaled and sank deep into the chair, her muscles going rubbery with fright.

Quay trotted the big blue roan out of town about five that afternoon, headed in the direction of the Willet ranch. The roan was a magnificently smooth striding animal — the best ride Quay had had since he rode a burro in Vegas a few weeks ago. Murphy's saddle was almost new, just broken in, and more comfortable than the old saddle he had traded Eskimo Jack.

He put the horse on the right road and gave him his head. Alternately the roan loped a while and walked a while. Once Quay touched him with a spur and the horse bolted into a dead run that almost left Quay behind. He had to grab the saddle horn and hold on until he could bring the horse back to a lope again. The rush of air past him almost tore his hat from his head. He laughed in pure delight. What a horse! He wondered where Robert got him. Neither he nor his friends had recognized the original name on the bill of sale, and the horse bore no brand.

Quay looked forward in eager anticipation to his visit to the Willet ranch, not as much for sitting at the well-stocked Willet table as for seeing Pearl again. He realized her beauty was beginning to haunt him, for she was the loveliest girl he had ever seen. But that wasn't all that attracted him to her: She was an intelligent girl who had both feet planted firmly on the ground. He did not believe she would ever let her intelligence interfere with common sense.

Certainly a vast amount of common sense — and all the deductive powers he could muster — were required of him right now. As he loped through the sagebrush flats outside of Reynaldo, he ran the things he had learned through his mind, trying to unravel not only the mystery of Robert Murphy's death but also to tackle what was beginning to form in his mind as a vastly greater problem for the whole area. Something was going on, something drastic and deadly that was beginning to affect all the people of Reynaldo and the surrounding countryside.

It was a magnificent countryside, too. Far away to his right, the mountains reared their majestic heads into the clear blue sky, soaring peaks of the Southern Rockies, sentinels standing guard over a vast terrain, mottled and broken by huge networks of canyons and badlands, providing enough range for thousands of cattle and sustenance for hundreds of people.

Coming from the more comfortable and regimented East, he had never known people such as these. They were violent folk, he thought, and then he tempered that: I am not a violent man, he said to himself, and I find that I have a kinship with these people. Neither are they violent — until violence directed toward them dictates their actions. He knew it had not been long since this country was wrested from the Indians, and certainly violence was necessary to do that. Many of those people had also been caught up in the bloody Lincoln County Cattle War and had borne arms to fight for what was theirs and to affect the peace. Brute force had been their next-door neighbor for years, and the current problems were not beyond their ability to handle — provided someone could ascertain what the problems were.

The current unrest had begun with the killings of Robert Murphy and Old Man Titlow. Why were they murdered, and how did their killings tie together? There must be a common denominator, Quay thought, but what was it? Perhaps the answer lay in subsequent events.

The cowboys from the Rocking R had discovered that seven people were present at the killing of Robert Murphy. An Indian, apparently an Apache, had visited Titlow the afternoon he was killed. Murphy had mentioned an Indian. Pearl had said that two men applied for work at the Willet ranch, and one was an Indian. Were these three Indians the same man? Was the Indian one of the seven who had killed Murphy?

Robert Murphy had hidden two weeks at the Willet ranch. Why? From whom?

Two new hands had gone to work for the Lazy G:

Arapaho Joe Davis and Spider Wellman. Davis was a killer from Texas. And Wellman had been eager to fight Quay. Why? Because Quay had found him talking with Rattler Baines, a notorious gunman? There were also two new hands at the Rocking R, Fairly and Johnson. Could this be coincidence, that men would apply for work at three ranches at the same time, two to each ranch? Quay thought it could be coincidental because word of a belated roundup had circulated, and cowboys who needed work were attracted. Would the presence of the Indian among them indicate something sinister? Quay wrestled with his Eastern-trained mind and finally decided it would not. There were still scattered trouble spots, especially in Apache country, but for the most part the Indian problem was under control.

There were more strangers than these in the country. Seltry had discovered tracks of a group of riders apparently hiding in the hills. Why? Who? Could they be riders with no connections here, taking refuge from the law. That was entirely plausible. But it could also be a wrong assumption.

The Clodhopper had been seen in Reynaldo, but only once, as far as Quay knew. He might simply have been passing through. Much of the Western population was transient, men living a hand-to-mouth existence, some working their way to a faraway place where fortunes might be better, others looking for an easy if unlawful touch.

He himself had been warned by at least two friends to start carrying a gun, and one had felt so strongly he had given Quay a gun. The rifle was in the saddle boot at this moment. He had never pointed a gun at another human being, and on the only occasion in which he might have used the gun, he had discarded it and resorted to his fists. Could he use the rifle, could he pull the trigger on another man, even if his life depended on it? Self-preservation is one of man's strongest instincts, yet he honestly didn't know whether he could kill another human being.

Possibly what disturbed him most, and seemed to link one thing to another, though he didn't know exactly what, was his discovery of Arapaho Joe and Wellman in serious conversation with Rattler Baines. He shuddered to think what would have happened to him had Zeb Willet not chanced to come by. Or was it something other than chance that had brought him by?

His thoughts rambled on. He had found Murphy's horse,

but who was the little man with no front teeth who had traded the horse to Eskimo Jack? And where did he get the horse? He might have been one of the seven — or he might have caught up a loose saddlehorse on the range.

Then there were today's wanton killings of Grafton Tumbler and Big John Radcliff, which would have to sorely weaken the leadership of the Tumbleweed ranch. The way the killings were described to him, one must attach more than spur-of-the-moment anger to the murders, especially since Rattler Baines had pulled the trigger.

Finally, he thought of the steer hide with the altered brand that Willet had brought to town, showing the Willet "W" changed to a WXL. There had been more than one steer with changed brand, Willet had said. The steers had come from the upper range, not unreasonably far from where Seltry had seen the tracks of the mysterious riders.

Quay thought back over the things he had tolled off in his mind. Were these unrelated events? Or did they tie together somehow? Some, he decided, were probably unrelated, but all could not be coincidental. Something was going on, and he felt he had the key to the puzzle. He only needed to unlock it. He also felt that Robert had had the key and had known what the answers were. Had he realized the danger he was in? If so, why hadn't he left at least a clue for Quay?

That was it! He would have left something for Quay — some information, some proof, a piece of the puzzle. Robert was like that. He had an analytical mind.

That was a sobering thought. If anyone else was thinking the same thing, he might be in deeper trouble than he had begun to suspect. Warily he swept his gaze through the country around him, but he saw no other living soul — just cattle, hundreds of cattle. He was amazed at the size of the plume of dust behind him, kicked up by his loping horse's hooves. It was so large that anyone within miles could see him coming and observe the direction in which he was riding. If any of the Willets were out of the basin, they knew by now that he was on the way. Or that someone was on the way.

Where would Robert have left something for him? It would be in an obvious place, a place that Quay was fairly sure to find. Where?

He looked upward and raised his hands.

"Where, Robert?" he screamed. "Where?"

"Right here, kid!" a faraway voice answered, and Quay reacted by pulling back on the reins.

The blast of a rifle shattered the afternoon and Quay felt a jolt — more of a jerk, really, as the heavy slug glanced off his saddle horn. He didn't have time to look at the horn, nor at the jumble of rocks where the shot came from. Dagger reacted with incredible speed, exploding in a rush that almost left Quay behind and then carried him along the road at breakneck speed.

Another slug snapped by his ear, and he recovered his senses, leaning over the saddlehorn, giving his assailant as small a fleeing target as possible.

In a moment of headlong flight, the great horse carried him out of rifle range. When he heard no more slugs passing, he pulled gently on the reins and the horse decreased speed. Quay twisted in the saddle and looked back but saw nothing unusual. No one was in sight. Only the rocks and sandy soil and dust, a few scattered mesquites, and clear blue sky.

He pulled the horse to a stop and let him blow. So badly was he shaking from fright that he could barely hold himself in the saddle. Someone had actually tried to kill him. He pulled his own rifle out of the scabbard and carried it in his hands the rest of the way to the Willet ranch.

He was still pale when he rode into the Willet place and Pearl met him in the yard.

"Quay!" she exclaimed. "I thought you were Robert. You're riding his horse."

"We found it," he said sharply, causing her to look at him more closely.

"Why, Quay, what's wrong with you? You're pale as death."

"Someone shot at me," Quay said, almost falling off the horse, "several times."

She was horrified. "Are you all right? Did they hit you?"

"No, they missed, and I'm all right, but my knees are still knocking."

"You poor man," she said. "Put your horse in the corral and come on in. Father and the boys will be in soon."

When his horse was cared for, she led him to the porch and seated him in the shade, listening to his story of how he was mysteriously shot at. His hands were still shaking slightly.

"I'm so sorry," she said, and there was sympathy in her voice. "We've both had difficult afternoons." She told him of the visit of Rattler Baines and how she got the drop on him and forced him off the ranch, and he paled further.

"Pearl, what if he returns?" he asked with fear ringing in his voice.

"He won't come back," she said, "not after the way he left. He would be too embarrassed."

"Maybe," Quay said, "but you can't be sure. It would be better if you weren't left alone here any more."

Willet and his sons rode in before sundown, coming from the direction Quay had arrived. The lines in Willet's face were deepened by weariness.

"Howdy, young man," he called to Quay. "Be with you in a minute. Let us get unhitched here."

The three unsaddled their mounts and slung saddles and blankets over the top rail of the corral. "Let 'em air out awhile," Willet said. "We can put 'em up after supper."

He walked to the house and slumped in a chair on the porch. Quay took a chair beside him. "Well, what brings you out here, Mr. Quay, as if I couldn't guess?"

"You'd be right with your guess," Quay laughed. "Pearl invited me to supper. I hope you don't mind."

"No, no, not atall. You're welcome anytime. Tell me what you've found out about your friend. I see you're ridin' his horse. Where'd you find it? Did it show up off the range?"

Quay explained how he had obtained ownership of the horse.

Willet laughed hard. "Say, that's all right. Anybody who can pull one over on Eskimo Jack is goin' some, I reckon. How about handin' me that bottle out of the kitchen. I'm about tuckered."

Quay went to the kitchen and Pearl, busy with pots and pans, handed him a quart bottle of white whiskey and a glass of water. Willet pulled long at the bottle, smacked his lips, and washed the fiery liquid down with a draught of water.

"Now that's good," he said, contentedly. "Friend of mine's got a good still back in the Sacramentos. Keeps me supplied, but I don't use it except when I'm tired like this."

"You've put in some time since you were in town today," Quay observed.

"Yes, I have, and the boys have, too. We're bunchin' steers on the flat for the drive next week. Got to have five hundred down there by Monday. That's four days from now. Tall order."

"Can I help?" Quay asked.

"You ever punched cows?"

"No, but you could show me what to do."

"Well, now, I might take you up on that sometime, but not right now. Bustin' cows out of the brush ain't exactly the easiest way to learn."

"I don't mind hard work," Quay said. "If I could help you, I'd be happy."

"Sounds like you've got your hands full with your own work," Willet responded. "I reckon me an' Zeb an' Ray can make do. We got about three hundred down there now. Ask me again when you find out what happened to your friend, an' I'll shore learn you to punch cows."

"You say you're driving Monday?" Quay asked.

"Yep. All four of us ranches along here will throw five hundred head apiece down on th' flats by Monday. On Tuesday morning, we've named a combined crew — four men from each ranch — that's sixteen in all — will drive 'em to Roswell. The buyer'll take 'em off our hands there."

"But there aren't four hands on your ranch."

"No, we're only sendin' two, me an' Zeb. The Rockin' R and Lazy G will chip in an extra man apiece for the drive. It'll shore be like old times."

"Old times?"

"I went up the trail a few times to Abilene, once all the way to Montana, with trail herds. Been some time ago, eighteen, nineteen years. But it's still in my blood. Ain't ever seen times like them again."

"You trailed cattle to Abilene?"

"Right up th' trail. Nothin' stopped us — not storm or flood or stampede, not Indians or Jayhawkers. Time or two we fit our way through. I went four times, best I recollect, an' we took twenty-five hundred steers every time. Reckon I helped move ten thousand head to Kansas an' beyond."

"Will you boss this drive?"

"No. Junior Wayburn's gonna take it. He went up the trail, too, maybe more times than I did. He's a good man in the saddle and a respected man by everybody. He's the best man for the job. I'm goin' as a trail hand, same as before."

He looked away into the distance, and Quay knew he was there on the Texas plains again, driving cattle in retrospect. He hated to break the old man's reverie, but he wanted to know about the drive.

"How're you going?" he asked.

"Why, straight down the road to Roswell," Willet said.

"We'll cross Salt Creek and ford the Pecos, but that ain't much of a job this time of year."

"That ought to be a sight to see," Quay said. "How'll you get all the cattle together?"

"Oh, Junior'll start at the Tumbleweed, bring their's down to his'n, pick them up, an' come on here. We'll throw mine in the herd and drive down to the Rockin' R, pick up theirs, and head for Roswell. Not many around here ever saw a herd of that size on the move. It *will* be somethin' to see, boy, it shorely will."

Zeb and Ray drifted up from the barn, and while the four washed for supper, Zeb asked, "What ripped your saddlehorn? Looks like a bullet gash."

Quay told the Willet men what had happened on the trail, and John Willet thought long and hard, staring at Quay. Finally, he said, "Mr. Quay, I hope you've still got the other half of a round-trip ticket out here and back. It's time you headed home. You know you're in over your head."

"I know I am," Quay said, "and I've thought about going home, but I still don't know what happened to Robert. I'm beginning to get more than a little mad. I don't think Robert had done anything to deserve being killed the way he was, and I *know* I haven't. So what's going on? I wish somebody would tell me. How about you, Mr. Willet? Are you sure you don't know something you're not telling me?"

"Boy, if I did, I ain't sure I'd tell you. But I don't, an' that's God's truth. You're into somethin' here that might be better for you if you went home with questions on your mind. I hope you don't stay out here and die learning the answers."

"You really should spend more time worrying about your daughter," Quay said, hoping his words would not anger Willet. "Rattler Baines paid her a visit this afternoon after he killed Tumbler and Radcliff in town."

"What?"

Pearl composed her voice and gave her father and brothers the details of her run-in with the outlaw chieftain.

"I don't think he'll be coming back," she concluded. "He tucked his tail between his legs and ran like a rabbit."

"No matter," Willet reached a quick conclusion, "until this thing is settled, we won't leave you alone here again. One of the boys will stay with you from now on."

"Now, father, you have your work. . . ." she began, but he raised a hand and hushed her.

"It's settled," he said. "We might take chances with them cows down there, but we won't take chances with you, Pearl."

There was gratitude in her eyes, but still she protested weakly.

"But I don't think he'll be coming back."

"Why not, daughter?"

"Because I told him I'd kill him if he came here again."

"And would you, daughter?"

"Yes, Father," she replied, lowering her eyes. "There are few people I believe I could kill, but he is one of them."

"No matter," her father said. "You won't have to do that."

It was still light when supper ended, and when Pearl finished cleaning up the kitchen, she suggested they walk out to the corral and look at the horses.

Quay's blue roan stood taller than the other horses. Most were mustangs, caught in the wild by Zeb and Ray and broken here in the riding corral.

"That's my favorite," she pointed to a pinto mare. She had good lines. "Zeb caught her in the hills beyond Coldwater Canyon, and she was so gentle we didn't have to break her. We thought she might have belonged to someone and escaped and turned wild."

"She's a beauty," Quay said, and then he looked off toward the brooding hills in the east. "Something's up there, Pearl — something or someone. I have the feeling that the answers I'm searching for may lie in those hills."

Although the valley was now in deep shadow, sunlight still glanced off the high hills, and its waning light turned them to gold and vermillion and purple, all mottled with the blackness of the pine forest.

As the sunlight faded off the peaks, stars began to appear above them, and the two stood transfixed as if lost in another world. At that moment, Quay's entire world seemed to center on the Willet ranch — at least on this dark-haired beauty standing beside him.

Lamplight shown eerily from the windows of the house, and in the corral a horse stamped and snorted, bowing its neck and crow-hopping into a trot around the corral. A colt came out of the barn on wobbly legs and Quay and Pearl laughed as it tentatively explored the corral, sniffing at the fence posts, the snubbing post in the center, and at clods of manure around the lot.

"Pearl, I'm thinking I'm the luckiest man in the territory, finding you like I did," he suggested, and smiling, she moved nearer.

"How come one of these locals hasn't taken you away on his steed and married you?" he asked, sincerely puzzled. "You're certainly beyond marriageable age."

She laughed again.

"I'm not prying," he added quickly, "just wondering."

"I'm twenty-two," she said, "and some of the local boys have tried to whisk me away, but the right one hasn't come along. A lot of them came courting. They brought me candy, and some picked flowers out on the desert and brought them to me. One even brought me a rabbit in a box. I admired all of them, and I went to a dance or two in town with some of the nicer cowboys, but not any of them really appealed to me."

"I'm glad," he could think of nothing else to say.

"Dad's afraid I'll be an old maid," she laughed. "He never came right out and said so, and I don't really think he wants to get rid of me. I'm too good a cook. But he'd like me to marry some cowhand — I can tell that — and live on the ranch so he can have the best of two worlds: grandchildren and good cooking."

The music of her laugh brightened the ranch yard, and Quay marveled again at her beauty, her personality, her great sense of humor, at everything about her. She was a girl filled with pluses; he could think of no minuses he could apply to her.

Quay kissed her, and she responded, slipping her arms around his neck. Hungrily, he kissed her again and she moved her body against his. He felt her breasts pressing against him, felt the light touch of her hair as he ran his fingers through it. There, lost in time and place, they stood as one on an island in the midst of a sea of mesquite and juniper and sage.

"Oh, Quay," she pulled away from him. "Quay, let's not do something we'd be sorry for."

"No," he said, "not now. Not here. I'm sorry. I didn't mean to be so forward."

"It isn't that," she said. "I just don't want to do something that might come between us later."

As her words sank in, Quay realized she had included him in her future. He was overcome with joy. To think that this beautiful girl, the loveliest girl he had ever known, had feelings for him was almost beyond his imagination at this point. He almost wept.

"Shhhh," she moved back into his arms, daubing with a handkerchief at his eyes.

They stood lost in time, and above them the stars moved slowly. Full darkness came upon the valley, and the screen door creaked at the house.

"Pearl," her father called. "Pearl, are you out here?"

"Here, Father," she answered. "By the corral."

"It's late."

She took Quay by the hand and walked slowly toward the house, relishing this time together, and she realized she had been wishing it would never end.

"Quay," she said, "I. . . I think a lot of you."

"Yes," he said. "I know. I can't explain it, but Pearl, I love you, too."

"Oh Quay," she melted into his arms again, and this time she didn't care if her father was still on the porch peering into the darkness.

Quay woke with the dawn and heard sounds in the kitchen. Easing out of bed, he cracked the door of his room and heard Pearl humming while she cooked breakfast. Quickly he dressed, and taking razor and soap went to the back porch. He was surprised that a pan of warm water awaited him there. He lathered and shaved. Brushing his thick hair back, he looked again in the mirror hanging on a post, and laughed. He realized he was suddenly happier than he had been since childhood, even with the shadow of Robert Murphy's death hanging over him. He had never really been in love, but he knew he had been smitten this time.

Still, he mustn't let newfound love interfere with his thinking process. He still had Robert's death to solve, and for the first time he began to feel that he had made progress. He must have progressed, otherwise why should someone shoot at him? Whoever killed Robert must think Quay knew more than he did.

Somehow, he must tie the incidents of the past few days together. He had little doubt that they were not intertwined. But where should he look next?

His gaze roamed off toward those brooding hills to the east, up above the rim of the basin, and he felt pulled to them. He had had the same feeling last night, standing with Pearl at the corral before he had been swept up in the moment of their first kiss.

A compulsion overcame him to ride back into the hills, farther than he had gone the first time, and determine what seemed to be calling him to them. He had never before experienced such a feeling and had no explanation for it. Perhaps his mind was playing tricks. He thought about that, standing in the early morning sun, and discarded the notion. It was not his mind; it was those mysterious riders Clingman Seltry had seen!

Answers lay there. He knew it! There was no more doubt. He would ride into the hills and explore until he found the answers.

The Willet men had left before dawn to complete their roundup. Pearl had his breakfast on the table when he walked back in the house.

"Don't let it get cold," she said as he kissed her gently on the cheek.

He sat down and began to eat.

"Pearl," he said hesitantly, "I'm going to ride back in the hills this morning. I can't shake the feeling that what I'm looking for is there."

"Oh, Quay, it could be dangerous if there is a gang hiding up there. And it isn't an easy ride."

"I know. I've been before, remember? But I must go. I'll be all right."

"I'm going with you," she said, and when he protested he found there was nothing he could say to change her mind.

They saddled up when he finished breakfast. She saddled the pinto mare and he tightened the girth of Robert Murphy's saddle beneath the belly of the blue roan.

The sun lay warm upon the land, though the day wouldn't heat fully until they were deep in the pine forest where it would be cooler than here in the valley. From the rim of the basin, he looked back and saw the sun twinkling off the windows of the Willet ranchhouse. His eyes swept the basin but he saw no other person, just cattle, most of them mere dots on the landscape. Far off he saw a darker area that he took to be the Willet cattle bunched on the flat.

Somewhere in the hills were the Willet men, rousting cattle out of brush-choked ravines, sweating, slaving for their living.

He enjoyed the morning. It was a beautiful day, and here beside him rode the woman he loved. What more could he ask? He thought about that a moment and knew he could ask for the answers he sought to the worst riddle he had ever tackled. Nothing in his classes at Yale had prepared him for anything like he was experiencing. This was life — real, unvarnished life, replete with pleasure, fettered with hardship, danger, and heartbreak.

He watched Pearl sway to the movements of the pony ahead of him. She wore a split skirt and rode a man's saddle, knowing it would be safer if they suddenly had to ride hard and fast. Indeed, he thought, she was a beautiful woman from any angle. She carried a Winchester rifle in the saddle boot, and he had no doubt she could use it as good as almost any man.

Presently they struck the steep mountainside and he took the lead, carefully guiding the horses the way he had ridden the first time he came up here, angling off to the north. He recognized the stream when they came to it, and turned Dagger up the mountainside beside the stream, knowing the big horse could make the grade easily. Pearl's pinto had no trouble keeping up, scrambling in places where the earth gave way under the weight of the horses.

In late morning they came to the hidden mountain valley he had found on his previous trip, and he led her through the woods and over a hump, avoiding the game trail. She caught her breath at the site of the pastoral park. "Quay," she exclaimed, "it's a lovely place."

"I found it the first time I came here," he said. "Look. There're the ashes of my campfire."

They watered the horses at the stream, stripped them of saddles and bridles, and turned them loose in the grass, knowing they would not stray.

Pearl removed a wrapped parcel from her saddlebags and said, "Lunch."

Together they ate, enjoying each other's company. He pointed to the ridge that ran above the secret cave, told her exactly how to get to the cave, and promised he would show it to her when they rode on.

Relaxed, he settled back, head on his saddle. The sun was warm on his chest and a whisper of a breeze floated through the meadow. Never had he felt so contented. Looking over the park, he saw that the horses were grazing contentedly. His eyes closed but he forced them open again, not wanting to appear sleepy to Pearl. She laughed. "Go ahead and rest," she said softly. "You must be exhausted."

He smiled, settled his head on the saddle again, and closed his eyes.

Voices woke him. Male voices.
"Hey, look at that hoss!"

"Shore, I've seen it before."

"It's mine. That's the hoss I sold in town. What's he doin' up here?"

"Let's get him."

They came onto the meadow out of the trees, four men riding abreast. One pulled his rope and shook out a noose, and just as they began to charge, Quay slipped his rifle from its scabbard and raised himself off the ground.

The riders saw him immediately and swiftly turned their horses toward him. He hesitated, not knowing what to do, and when he looked around for Pearl and saw that she and her horse were gone, it was too late to act. The noose settled over his shoulders and the rider stopped his horse, backing him away.

Tightening around Quay's shoulders, the rope pinned Quay's arms to his sides. He dropped the rifle and was jerked off his feet. The rider turned his horse and touched him with a spur and the horse moved away, dragging Quay through the grass.

"That's enough!" another rider commanded. "Cut it out, Handy."

"I know where he got his name," a third man said. "He's too handy with that rope."

Handy checked his horse, and Quay got to his feet, loosening the noose around him. The rope dropped to the ground and he stepped out of it.

"What is this?" he asked. "What's going on?"

The man called Handy rode back, recoiling his rope. "Where'd you get that hoss?" he asked, and Quay saw that he was a small man with close-set eyes and pinched features. He had no front teeth.

"I bought him," Quay said. "I have a bill of sale."

"Where'd you buy him?"

"I bought him from a man named Eskimo Jack in Reynaldo."

The others looked at Handy who finally broke into a toothless grin. "That's where I sold him, all right. Old Eskimo gimme twenty-five dollars for that hoss." He laughed aloud. "Maybe I can sell him to somebody else fer a hundred. He's worth ever' bit of it."

Quay moved back toward his rifle, but realized that two of the riders held rifles and both were pointed straight at him.

112

"I'd be mighty careful what I picked up, was I you," one said.

"What are you doing?" Quay asked. "I haven't done anything. What do you want?"

"Fer one thing," Handy said, "I want that hoss. I reckon you can sign the bill of sale over to me."

"That's my horse!" Quay said emphatically. "He's not for sale."

"Oh, he's fer sale, all right," Handy grinned, "one way or another."

"Mister, who are you and what are you doin' up here?" asked a big man with a note of authority in his voice.

"My name's John, uh, Jones," he lied.

"Jones, huh?" the spokesman laughed and looked at Handy. "Maybe you're some kin, Handy." He looked back at Quay. "You'll have to pick another name. Handy's already took Jones."

"That's my name," Quay said.

"Don't matter. What you doin' up here?"

"I'm riding," Quay explained, hoping they would believe his story. "I ride this way sometimes. I wanted to exercise my horse."

"Well, it's good exercise, all right, comin' up these hills, but I ain't satisfied. Handy, go catch up yore hoss an' we'll make some tracks. Mister, you're comin' with us."

"Now see here!" Quay ejaculated.

"No," the man said quietly. "*You* see here. One way or another, you're comin' with us. You can do it walkin' or draped over a saddle. Don't matter to me which."

The blue roan shied away from Handy's noose, walling his eyes and prancing, obviously nervous at the sight of this man.

"He knows you, Handy," one of the other men laughed.

"He ought to," Handy returned. "He's tasted this rope before."

He tossed the lasso and the noose settled heavily over Dagger's head. Handy gave the rope a vicious yank, and the horse snorted and reared in fear. Handy jerked it back down.

"Stand calm," the big man cautioned Quay. "Handy won't hurt him none. He just wants to show him who's boss."

Suddenly the horse charged and Handy tried to get out of the way, but the roan's big barrel chest struck Handy's shoulder and knocked him to the ground. Quick as a flash, two other ropes dropped over the horse's head, and the two riders pulled the roan to a halt. He stood trembling.

"I'll kill him!" Handy said, coming off the ground, favoring the shoulder the roan had hit. "I'll kill him dead!"

"Leave him be," the big man ordered. "I reckon the boys can handle him if you can't."

Handy glared at the man, but obeyed. He picked up his hat, clamped it on his head, and stomped back to his horse.

"Handy, get the man's saddle and put it on the roan," the big man said, and Handy glared at him again. But he obeyed. Held by the ropes, the roan stood still while Handy tightened the girth, and when Quay moved toward the horse the big man shook his head. "Keep your distance, mister. You can walk where we're goin'."

"Why should I walk?" Quay asked defiantly. "That's my horse."

"If I say walk, you walk," the man answered, "an' I say so. Git!"

One of the others led the roan, and Quay walked in the direction the man indicated, heading for the game trail that led around the hill of the secret cave.

As he neared the location of the cave, Quay studied the hill through narrowed eyes and thought he saw a movement in the brush. It was Pearl. It had to be! Quay prayed silently that she would remain still and unseen, and when he drew abreast of her position, he had an idea. He stopped and turned.

"Why can't I ride?" he demanded.

"Keep goin'."

"My feet are killing me in these boots."

"Sounds like a cowpuncher shore enough," one of the others laughed.

"Shut up, and keep goin'," the big man said. "It ain't far."

"How far?" Quay asked, knowing that Pearl — if that was really Pearl on the ridge — could hear every word.

"Maybe a mile. Maybe not that far. Move along now before I move you."

"I still don't know why I can't ride," Quay persisted.

"Mister, you might get away on that hoss," the big man said, "but you ain't goin' nowhere up here afoot, not in these mountains. Now shut up and go. I won't tell you again."

Quay read pure menace in the man's voice, and saw more in his eyes. They were gray and icy. Quay began to walk. He knew Pearl had heard it all and would know they weren't going far. Perhaps she could follow and help him escape. But as soon as the thought came, he discarded it. No. It would be far better if she went back to the ranch and got help. She was a sensible girl. That was exactly what she would do — and the Willet men would show these galoots a thing or two.

He picked up his stride, for the path was not steep. It wound between the ridge that held the cave and another parallel ridge. Trees closed around them and the forest was silent. Only the plodding of the horses broke the silence.

They came to a slash in the ridge to the left and the big man said, "In there."

Quay walked into a deep ravine, washed out eons of time ago by the stream that flowed past his meadow. His meadow? He might have laughed at the thought had his situation been less grave. Too, he knew he should pay attention to where they were going; so in his mind he marked every turn of the trail, every odd-shaped tree and stone. He shuddered to think that these might be the men who had killed Robert. That would explain how Handy came by Robert's horse. Of course, he could have found it wandering on the desert, but Quay doubted that.

The ravine was deep and long, perhaps a half-mile long, Quay thought, and when he was almost at the far end, the trail turned sharply to the left and a clearing loomed ahead.

"In there," the big man said, and Quay walked into the clearing.

Four other men rose to their feet as the party came into camp. Gear was strewn about, packs and saddles mostly. Bridles hung over a low limb on a tree. A coffeepot stood on a rock beside the coals of a fire, and beyond the fire were two tents, each large enough to sleep two or three men. The area was flat for a space of twenty yards or so, but the clearing was small, no larger than the flat. The creek ran along the edge of the flat.

"Howdy, Cling," one of the men in camp called. "See you brought company, an' we ain't even got the breakfast dishes washed. I wish you'd let us know when you're bringin' somebody home with you; we could clean up around here a little."

The big man did not join in the jocularity.

"Knock it off, Sam," he said, slipping off the horse. "Where's Garney an' the other boys?"

"In town, I reckon. Left right after you did. Said they

might not get back tonight. Me an' Jim an' Ranny here been thinking about taking off an' maybe going to town."

"That ain't smart," Cling said. "Better if they don't see too many strangers in town. You hang around here."

"Aw, ain't nothin' to do here," Sam complained. "Can't play no more cards. I done won ever'body's money." He chuckled.

"Then give it back and start over."

"Huh? You crazy?"

"Well, read a book."

"You know I can't read."

"Then shut up an' sit down."

Sam turned away and walked in the direction of the creek. Cling indicated a log and told Quay to sit on it.

"Want me to tie his hands?" Handy asked, hauling out a pigging string.

"No," Cling said. "He ain't goin' nowhere. He couldn't get a half a mile before we ran him down. Leave him be."

The afternoon drew on and Quay sat on the log. Occasionally he rose and walked around camp, stretching his leg muscles.

The man named Jim sat beside Quay on the log and in a low voice introduced himself. "My name's Jim Rafter," he said. "What's your's?"

"John Jones," Quay answered, and Rafter laughed.

"Well, John Jones, you got yourself in a mess. You get any chance at all, you better cut an' run. It ain't gonna be healthy around here for you, specially if anybody can connect you with that girl you was with in town the other day."

"What are you talking about?" Quay asked, dumbfounded that Pearl would be drawn into this.

"Just remember what I said," Rafter added. "You get a chance, cut an' run."

He rose and walked away, and Quay, puzzled, watched him go.

"What's in his saddlebags?" Quay heard Cling ask Handy, and Handy, digging in the bags, replied, "Little junk. No identification. He ain't got much. Few shells fer that Winchester. Hey, here's an old hogleg forty-four that'd blow a hole in the side of a barn. Couple'a books. That's about all."

Quay was glad he had put his money in the bank at Reynaldo. They had not found the few dollars he carried in his pocket; no one had searched him.

116

Off and on, he picked up bits of conversation, and once he heard Cling caution the men about talking around him. "Watch your tongues," he said sternly.

The men mentioned Garney several times, and Quay wondered who Garney was. Once he heard Sam ask a question of Cling in a low voice, and Cling replied, "Don't worry about it. Garney'll get him."

Get who? Quay wondered. Had Garney gone to town after someone. Was Garney meeting someone in town to bring here, or did the comment carry more ominous tones?

The man called Sam opened a pack in late afternoon and brought out a couple of pans. "I'll get somethin' fryin' here," he said. "How about chunkin' up the fire, Ranny?"

Ranny shoved several sticks of firewood into the coals and the fire flickered and caught. Presently the dry sticks began to burn with a bright flame. For the first time, Quay noticed a side of beef hanging from a limb behind the tents, and from this Sam cut a panful of thick steaks.

"We'll eat good tonight," he laughed, and Quay overheard him add, "thanks to Old Man Willet."

Quay thought the steak was delicious, and Sam was a hand at frying potatoes. He baked bread in a Dutch oven. Altogether the food was as good or better than that at the cafes in Reynaldo.

Quay thought about commenting on the food, hoping it would encourage conversation, but he didn't want to go too far. He didn't want anyone suspecting him of prying. Still, he thought, nothing ventured, nothing gained.

"My compliments to the chef," he said.

"Huh?" Sam looked at him quizzically.

"This is good food," Quay grinned.

"Ought to be," Sam said. "I learned to cook under the best old hambone on the Chis'um Trail. Name of Sorry Stokes. Everybody kidded him about how sorry his grub was, but he could throw it together, an' nobody on the trail ate better than we did."

"Shut up!" Cling commanded across the fire. "Leave him be. Tend to your cookin'."

"Just makin' conversation," Sam complained. "Nothin' else to do around here."

"Then don't do nothin'," Cling's voice grew stern. "Just shut up!"

The others spent the evening shunning Quay, not daring to risk Cling's ire. After a while, darkness settled over the hills. It crept into the glade as if someone had slowly pulled down the shades. Most of the men rolled smokes and someone shoved more sticks in the fire.

Quay counted only seven men. Cling sat off to himself, smoking silently, and presently he looked around, and asked, "Where's Handy?"

"Joe come in," Jim Rafter said, "and him and Handy walked off up the trail. Reckon they had to go to the woods."

"Go see if their horses are here," Cling ordered, and Rafter heaved himself to his feet and walked up the trail. Ten minutes later he came back.

"Hosses is gone," he said. "Both of 'em. Joe and Handy must've lit a shuck."

Cling's eyes narrowed and his brow clouded. "They get in trouble," he hissed, "I'll break their fool necks. I told 'em to stay here."

Ranny spread a blanket on the ground. Five of the seven remaining men sat crosslegged around it, and Quay heard the soft rustle of cards. Rafter pulled a quart of whiskey from his saddlebags, jerked out the cork with his teeth, and hefted the bottle to his lips, coughing and gagging when he removed it.

The others laughed. "Here," someone said, "let a man show you how to handle that stuff."

Cling glared at the group, but said nothing. Through the evening, the five lowered the level in the bottle steadily, and finally Ranny hurled the bottle down through the trees toward the creek, climbed clumsily to his feet, and found another quart.

"Better go easy on that stuff," Cling advised, but Ranny paid him no mind. During the next hour the five killed that quart, too, and one by one sought their soogans and soon began to snore.

The fire wore down and Cling came to Quay. "Hands behind your back," he said, showing Quay the pigging strings he carried.

"How can I sleep with my hands tied behind my back?" Quay asked.

"I don't care how you sleep," Cling said. "I just want you here in the mornin'."

He tied Quay's hands tightly, then spread a blanket on the ground away from the fire, near the base of a big cedar which had boughs almost touching the ground.

"Lay down here," he snapped, and when Quay dropped on the blanket, Cling bound his feet, and threw another blanket over him.

"Go to sleep," he ordered, and walked to one of the tents. Taking another long look at the snoring men sprawled in disarray around the fire, he shook his head in disgust and entered the tent.

After a few minutes, the other sober man, whose name Quay had not heard, rose and stretched, nodded at Quay, and went in the other tent. Minutes later, his snores joined those of the whiskey-laden men in a cacaphony of ungodly noise.

"I couldn't sleep anyway," Quay thought, and promptly went to sleep.

Quay awoke with a feminine hand over his mouth and soft lips pressing into his ear.

"Shhhh," he heard Pearl caution him to silence. She moved, and he felt a tug at the bonds binding his hands behind his back. In a moment, his hands were free. Another moment and she cut the cords holding his legs together.

Pulling gently on his shoulder, she rolled him over. Flexing his fingers to restore feeling to his numbed hands, he waited a moment to make sure no one else was awake, and then eased after Pearl, making certain he stepped on nothing that would make undue sound, and in that way they disappeared from camp into the darkness.

In the deep darkness of the forest, Pearl took his hand and led him up a trail of sorts. When they were away from camp, she moved near his ear again and whispered, "Stay with me. I've already saddled your horse."

"How in the name of? . . ." he didn't get his question finished, for she clapped her hand across his mouth again.

"Be quiet," she whispered. "There was no guard that I could find, but he may have been away from his post."

After that, they walked in silence, and his eyes gradually adjusted to the darkness until he could make out her form moving through the woods.

He heard the horses before he saw them, penned in a makeshift brush corral.

Swiftly they mounted and before they moved away, Quay leaned over and untied the rope that blocked the entrance to the corral. He turned the blue roan inside and silently hazed the other horses out.

Pearl turned away from camp, riding up the trail. The horses, pushed along by Quay, followed her pinto. A quarter mile away, Quay lashed at the horses' haunches with the ends of his reins and drove them off the trail. They scattered in the woods.

He nudged the roan alongside Pearl's mount.

"Thanks for breaking me free," he said. "How did you know where we were?"

"I was at the cave when you passed by. I overheard the big one say the camp wasn't far away, so I followed at a distance. I've been in the woods above camp all evening."

"What time is it?"

"About four in the morning," she said. "It's time we were making tracks."

"How do we get out of here?"

"The only way I know is to go around the camp and come back to the trail below it. I don't know where this trail goes and I'm afraid to follow it."

She reined off the trail and climbed through the brush to the south. After several minutes she turned west, walking her horse steadily through the woods.

Even though he couldn't see it, Quay sensed when they passed the camp. They were far enough above it not to disturb the sleeping men, and after ten more minutes of riding, Pearl reined the pinto down the hillside and back onto the trail.

The faint glow of early morning brightened the eastern sky and the two rode into the deep ravine. They were halfway through the ravine when they met the riders.

Four men slumped in their saddles, half asleep, coming toward Quay and Pearl with heads down. Quay recognized the figure of Handy Jones but couldn't tell who the others were in the early light.

Pearl reined in, desperately looking for a way of escape, but the walls of the ravine were too steep. They had to go back or go forward.

Pearl pulled her Winchester from the saddle scabbard, and Quay quickly unbuckled his saddlebag and withdrew the forty-four. Strapping the belt around his hips, he drew the pistol and said softly to Pearl, "They must be drunk. Let's go straight through them."

He kicked the roan in the sides and the big horse burst down the trail. Pearl came close behind him.

Before the riders could react, the two were upon them. The roan smashed into one horse and then another. Pearl fired the rifle in the air — and then they were free and running. Quay chanced a backward look and saw two riders down, their horses running up the trail. A third horse swung wildly around, spilling his rider beside the trail. The fourth fought for control of his half-wild mustang.

Quay and Pearl were two hundred yards away and riding fast before the four recovered. One pulled a pistol and snapped a couple of shots after the fleeing riders, but the shots weren't close.

The two rode hard for half a mile, then pulled in their mounts and slowed.

"We'd better head for the cave," Pearl shouted. "Those shots will bring the others."

"They're afoot," Quay returned. "Keep going."

But when their horses reached the area of the cave, Pearl jumped the pinto off the trail and onto a steep climb toward the cave. Quay had no choice but to follow.

They pulled up at the brush choking the cave.

"Let's get inside," Pearl said, excitedly.

The pinto shouldered its way through the brush and into the cave with Quay only a couple of lengths behind.

He protested. "We should keep going while we've got a lead."

"It's too far to the ranch," she said. "We'd never make it. They would either run us down or we might meet more of them on the trail. I'm sure they know shortcuts."

"How many are there? Who are they?" Quay asked.

"I don't know. I didn't know any of them, and there might be a dozen more. Who knows?"

Dismounting in the cave, they pushed the horses to the rear, and stepped back outside to listen. They heard no pursuit.

"Quickly," Pearl said, "gather some of this brush. We may need a light inside."

Each grabbed a handful of dead brush and carried it inside. With pigging strings, Quay bound the brush tightly into two torches, then joined Pearl outside again.

"I still think we should have kept going," he said.

"No. We're a long way from home. They might overtake us before we got there. We'd never be able to fight them off."

"Look," Quay pointed to the hillside where they had

scrambled up. The soil was ripped and torn by the hooves of their horses. "They won't have any trouble finding where we are."

A half-hour later, they heard horses approaching from the east. A half-dozen riders went by at a fast trot. Through the brush Quay saw Cling, Jim Rafter, Ranny, and Sam. Handy Jones was the fifth one, and the sixth was a stranger.

A moment later he heard a shout from down the trail.

"Hold up!"

"What's the matter?"

"We've run out of tracks," he heard Cling say. "They've turned off."

When they saw the riders coming back up the trail, Quay handed the heavy pistol to Pearl. "Give me your rifle," he said. "I couldn't hit anything with this."

"I can shoot it," she said.

"We're in a bind," he whispered in her ear. "I'm going to shoot to kill."

"Oh, Quay," he thought there were tears in her eyes when she spoke, "can you?"

"You bet I can," he said. "They'll kill *us* if we don't."

"I'll take the big one and Handy Jones," he pointed out the two to her. "You get someone else."

He waited, peering through the brush. Ranny had dismounted and walked in front of the others, studying the trail. When he came to the place where they jumped their horses off the trail, he stopped and looked around, finally discovering the tracks dug heavily into the hillside by their climbing horses.

He pointed. "They went this way. They're up there."

Quay's first shot struck Cling squarely in the chest. He levered the rifle and shot Handy Jones out of his saddle. The forty-four boomed at his side and he saw Sam go down. The others scattered and he slammed two more shots after them without scoring.

Sprawled in the trail, neither Cling nor Handy Jones moved. Quay was sure they were dead. Sam tried to rise and Quay shot him, putting him down for keeps.

"Back in the cave," he whispered and Pearl crawled backward. He followed.

His adrenalin was flowing faster than it ever had in a football game. This was a game of life and death — not only his death, but that of the beautiful girl beside him. He had felt a certain squeamishness after bruising opponents in football games, but, oddly enough, he felt no remorse for the dead men lying in the trail below, not even for Sam, who had apparently tried to befriend him in the outlaw camp. He had taken lives that were attempting to take his and the girl's, and there seemed to be a certain fairness in such transaction. Was it an eye for an eye and a tooth for a tooth? Of that he wasn't sure, but he was strangely calm.

In a moment a searching rifle fire broke from below. The remaining men were shooting through the brush and their shots struck the mountain above the cave.

There were three men left, none of them wounded. And when Quay considered their options against three armed men, he found them wanting. He could remain here, pinned down, until more help arrived for the bandits below. He could go out and stalk them. The thick brush would conceal him until he got near them. He discarded that option quickly; he was no stalker. He had never been a good game hunter. His third option was going deeper into the cave to see if he could find a way out. He could tell that the cave went deeper into the mountain.

It was only a matter of time before the shots found the cave opening, and Quay knew they must either improve their position or get out of there. He stepped to the opening and fired twice through the brush to let their assailants know they were still here.

"We're in trouble," he said to Pearl. "They'll find the cave for sure, and we have nothing to barricade this opening with."

"Maybe we can hold them off till dark," Pearl answered.

"I doubt it, and they'll be reinforced as soon as the rest round up their horses. Besides, if they find this opening, they'll kill our horses for sure. We've got to get out."

"But how?"

"I'm going to explore that passageway," he said, pointing to the opening in the rear of the cave. "It may lead somewhere. You fire the pistol now and then. There's a box of shells in my saddle bag. They won't rush us till the others come."

Striking a match, he lit one of the torches. It flared and caught and he moved into the opening. Almost immediately the passageway opened into a cavern so large the glow of his light fell short of the far side. He could hear running water but could not see it.

In the glare of the torch, he saw a huge spiderweb in the passageway, the largest he had ever seen. Barring his way, it stretched from the top of the passage to the bottom, anchored to rocks on both sides. An enormous spider glared at him with bright eyes reflecting the flickering light of his torch. He stared at the web in wonder. It must be ten feet tall, he thought, and even wider. As he looked at it, an eerie feeling came over him and the thought occurred like a shock: *This whole affair, this mystery of what happened to Robert Murphy is as tangled as that spiderweb.* Without further hesitation, he touched the web with the torch and the spider fled. He moved the torch in a circle, burning away the web, and quickly passed through.

Finding easy footing and sufficient room to get the horses through — if he could find a way out — he moved swiftly along. Queer formations appeared before him but he found a way through. At the far end of the cavern, several openings offered themselves to him. He chose one and passed through it into a large tunnel. Huge stalactites reached down from the low ceiling of the cave. Making sure he marked his path when he passed splits in the passageway, he continued and soon came to another arena larger than the first. He made a more difficult passage here, but thought they could still get the horses through.

The torch was half consumed and panic rose in his throat. He had not found an exit and if the torch burned out he could never find his way back in utter darkness.

Almost immediately when he passed through this cavern he saw light at the end of a short tunnel to his left. The horses could scramble into the passageway, he thought, working around a mass of stalagmites. He immediately turned and retraced his steps. Before he came back to the original cave he heard gunshots popping down the hillside and occasionally the louder boom of Pearl's forty-four.

He reached the cave just as his torch sputtered out. Sliding up beside Pearl, who lay at the cave entrance with the pistol in her hand, he peered into the brush and saw nothing.

"Quay, I think they're getting ready to rush us," she said. "Several men came down the trail a few minutes ago, and I've heard them talking."

"We can get out back here," he said. "It'll be a tight squeeze in a place or two, but I'm sure we can get the horses through."

"How long will it take?"

"Maybe ten minutes. There are big caverns back there. They're so large my torch couldn't light them up. Let's give 'em a few more shots and go."

"Where does it come out?"

125

"I couldn't tell. The torch was burning low and I came back as soon as I saw daylight."

"Oh, Quay, we may be getting into something we can't get out of."

"Even that," he said softly, "wouldn't be as bad as getting caught here. Come! We must go quickly."

The rifles opened up again, and a slug came in the entrance and buried itself in the ceiling above them, showering bits of dirt.

"Let's move," Quay said. "We'll lead the horses. I'll go first with the torch. You stay just behind. We have to move fast. Don't drop back too far; they may follow us quickly."

She gathered the reins of the pinto, and he stepped to the entrance and levered three fast shots into the brush. They were answered with a fusillade from below. Quay lit the other torch, scrambled to the blue roan, and hurried into the tunnel, pulling the horse behind him. In the first passage, he paused and asked, "Are you all right, Pearl? Can you see?"

"Go on," she said urgently, "I can keep up."

He went on, passing the first cavern, finding the second passageway. In less time than it had taken before when he picked his way carefully, he came to the second cavern and in the dim, flickering light immediately spotted the opening he wanted. He relaxed a bit, knowing anyone entering the cave behind them could no longer see the light of his torch. Once he paused to listen for pursuit but heard nothing. Gingerly, the horses picked their way around the stalagmites, pointing for the daylight Quay could see ahead. Scrambling up a short incline, they entered the final passage.

"Hurry," Pearl urged. "I thought I heard something back there."

Nearing the entrance, Quay threw down the torch and stomped it out.

"We're almost out," he said to Pearl. "We can make it."

They emerged in daylight on the back side of the ridge. Pearl surveyed the ravine below them and found it unfamiliar.

"Let's go that way," she pointed to the right, westward. "That's the direction we need to go."

Both stepped into their saddles and Quay let the roan pick its way down the ridge to the floor of the ravine. It was a wash, tumbled with rocks, but a faint trail led away to the west and they struck out immediately.

They could hear no sound of firing from the other side of the ridge, and they didn't pause to see if anyone came out of the opening above them.

"We'll get away," Quay said. "They wouldn't think to follow us in there with their horses. If they do come through, they'll be afoot."

He kicked the roan into a gallop, rode out of the ravine and onto a trail.

"Let's go," Pearl said quickly. "This will take us home."

The trail was good, and they made fast time, pausing occasionally to survey their backtrail and let their horses blow. By the time they reached the hills from which the great upland stretched below them, they were sure they had left pursuit behind.

Still, they skedaddled, riding down the trail side by side, for now it was the broad trail leading from Coldwater Canyon.

The sun had westered and was half below the horizon when they reached the rim of the basin in which lay the Willet ranch. Below, the valley was bathed in shadow, but they could see the ranch buildings. Pearl touched the pinto with her heels and it moved on down the trail. Quay and the blue roan followed.

The door of the ranchhouse burst open when they arrived at the corral and Willet came out.

"Daughter!" he shouted, running to the corral. "Daughter! Are you two married?"

She looked at him in astonishment. "Married? Whatever gave you that idea?"

"You've been gone since yesterday," he said. "Me and Zeb thought you'd run away to get married."

"Why on earth would we do that?" she asked, and Quay made every attempt to stifle a laugh.

"Well, you're both sweet on each other," Willet said. "That's plain as day."

"Father!" she stamped her foot, demanding silence. "Quay has been captured by outlaws. I helped him escape, and we spent most of today fighting them and getting away."

"What?"

"I'm too tired to stand here and talk about it," she said. "Come on inside. We'll tell you everything."

Together, Pearl and Quay related the events of their two-day ordeal. The Willets listened, asking occasional questions.

"And you killed three of 'em?" Willet asked.

"I didn't want to," Quay answered, "but I had no other choice."

"I shot one," Pearl said. "I knocked him down and Quay finished him."

"Daughter!"

"If we hadn't shot them," she said softly, "they would have killed us. We could never have held off all of them."

"Who were they?" Willet asked.

"We don't know," Quay answered, "except that they're a gang that has been hiding in the hills for some time. I heard about them at the Lazy G."

"They must be up to something," Willet said. "You got any idea what?"

"No," Quay thought about it for a moment, then said, "except that they must be tied in with the things that have happened in the valley. They're probably the ones who changed your brands. One of them claimed Robert's horse — my horse — and said he had sold it to Eskimo Jack. He could probably answer some questions for us, but unfortunately, he was one of those I shot."

"You got no hint of who they are or what they're doing? Think, man."

Quay ran the events through his mind again, pausing to ferret out any information that might be helpful.

"One of them said he'd been up the trail with herds," Quay said. "He was a cook named Sam. He was right friendly and I hated to kill him back there, but he was coming after us with a rifle. He mentioned going up the trail as a helper for a cook named Sorry Stokes."

"Sorry Stokes!" Willet ejaculated. "I remember Sorry Stokes. He was a good man, too. I remember a boy named Sam helpin' him. Sam Baines, his name was. He quit trail-drivin' and fell in with a gang of Jayhawkers who tried to steal everybody's cattle. They lived off other people's cattle for three or four years. Last I heard of him he was runnin' from the law with a brother, but I can't remember the brother's name."

"Could they have called him Rattler?"

"Could have. I don't know. It'd seem to fit, wouldn't it? Rattler Baines killed Grafton Tumbler an' John Radcliff for no apparent reason. All this must be tied in together. If we could find the handle, we could solve it maybe."

"Another thing that might help," Quay said, "the leader

of the pack seems to be a man they called Garney. Does that mean anything to you?"

"Garney what?" asked Willet.

"That's all they called him, Garney," Quay said.

"Garney? I don't know any Garney," Willet turned the name over in his mind several times and shook his head. "Beats me."

There was nothing left to talk about.

"Well, we're glad you two are back," Willet said, rising, "and we're a mite disappointed you didn't run away an' get married. You could do a whole lot worse, Pearl."

"Father!"

Quay chuckled. "Mr. Willet, I've been thinking a lot about what you're talking about, and now seems to be as good a time as any to ask for your daughter's hand."

Ray and Zeb exchanged knowing looks, and smiles crossed their faces. But Pearl rose quickly from her chair, put her fists on her hips, and faced Quay. "You might ask what I think about that," she stormed, but all four men could see that her defiance was mock anger.

"Well, I meant to mention it to you," Quay said, "but it came up so suddenly here that I thought. . . I. . . well. . . ."

"Well, what?"

"Hush, girl," Willet said. "You've both got my blessing. Work it out amongst yourselves. I think it's a right smart idea." He looked at the clock on the wall.

"Better get to bed, boys. It's nine-thirty, and we've got to finish pushing them cows down on the flat. We drive day after tomorrow."

Willet started to leave, then turned back to Quay. "Son, I told you night before last that you ought to pack up and head home, but I've changed my mind. We need men like you out here. You may be a little green, but you're learning." To Pearl he said, "We ate, but there ain't a lot left. You two must be hungry."

"Don't worry, Father, we'll find something."

The three left the room, and Quay looked at Pearl with trepidation, but her face broke into a broad smile and she came into his arms.

"Oh, Quay."

"Will you marry me, Pearl? I know we haven't known each other that long, but I feel as if I've known you all my life."

"What about your schooling, Quay?"

"I only have one year left," Quay said. "We can go east

while I finish — or we can stay here a while and I'll finish when I can."

"But your family. What will they think?"

"When they meet you," he grinned, "they won't be able to think of anything else. Will you marry me?"

"Yes, Quay. Yes, I will. As soon as you want me to."

"Then we'll find a preacher right after the drive."

She snuggled her body closer to him, and he tipped her chin upward and kissed her.

"Did you notice what Father said?" she asked.

He had no idea what she was talking about.

"What?" he asked.

"That's the first time he called you *Son*."

Quay's thoughts were so mixed he couldn't get to sleep. He thought of Pearl and her loveliness, and of the man named Garney. Who could he be? What was his purpose in moving a gang — apparently a gang of vicious killers — into the valley? Who could they be after?

One question disturbed him more than the others. Why would the outlaw named Jim caution him about mentioning his connection with Pearl? She had nothing to do with all this. A horrible thought flashed through his mind: Did they mean to do her harm? Was that the warning implied by the outlaw's words?

He had to find out who Garney was, and he determined that he would ride to Reynaldo early in the morning and ask there. Maybe Deputy Frazier would know.

Quay singlefooted the blue roan down the main street of Reynaldo early the next morning. He had felt safe enough riding into town alone. The big six-gun was packed away in his saddlebag, but a Winchester rifle Pearl had given him was at hand's reach in the saddle boot. He had lost the rifle Frazier had given him when the outlaws captured him in the meadow.

Reining over, he stopped the roan in front of the sheriff's office and tied it to the hitch rail. Frazier stepped out of the office and met him on the street.

"Where've you been? We've been mighty worried about you."

"Come inside," Quay said, "I need to talk to you."

Carefully choosing his words, he filled in the deputy on all that had transpired since he left town — how he was

131

shot at, how he was captured, how he had escaped, the killing of the three men. He omitted his asking Pearl to marry him.

"Sounds like a bunch of bushwhackers," Frazier said. "You're mighty lucky, young man, you and the girl, too."

"We know that," Quay returned, "but what's important right now is to find out who Garney is. He must be Rattler Baines. Can you wire the sheriff and ask?"

"Yeah, I reckon I can do that. I got to go down to the telegraph office anyway. Take a couple hours to get an answer back, if the sheriff's in. Longer if he ain't."

"We also need to determine what a gang of thieves would be doing here," Quay said. "Maybe the bank is expecting a lot of money. . . or could someone in town be receiving a shipment of goods expensive enough to attract scum of this sort?"

"I doubt it, but I can ask. It could be a raid on the bank, at that."

"I'll be over at the saddlemaker's," Quay said. "I want him to fix that bullet burn on my saddlehorn."

"That's a mighty handsome saddle," Frazier said. "I'd get it fixed, too."

Wilson, the leatherworker, was in the Rimrock Saloon, talking with Grayson. Quay explained what he wanted and the two went outside for Wilson to examine the saddlehorn.

"Sure, I can fix it," Wilson said. "Slip it off the horse and I'll take it on over to the shop."

Quay unsaddled the roan and Wilson left with the saddle. Quay turned the horse into the corral at the livery and went back uptown. He ate at a cafe and talked with a couple of hands from the Tumbleweed, who told him that despite the deaths of Tumbler and Radcliff their herd was standing ready, waiting for the drive the following morning. They also said they had seen the Lazy G herd on its bedground as they rode to town. Quay knew the Willets had their cattle ready, and figured the Rocking R was finishing up since Curly Ford, Gus Braswell, and Sheep Calahan were not in town.

The afternoon passed slowly. Before sundown he ate again and picked up his saddle at Wilson's. New leather covered the horn. Depositing the saddle in his hotel room, he walked down the street to the deputy's office, but Frazier wasn't around.

Quay felt fatigue from his all-night ordeal two nights

ago and decided he would eat, look for Frazier once more, and go to bed. He wanted to be out to the Willet bedground early for the start of the drive.

The nearest eating place was the cantina and Quay went there. When his eyes became accustomed to the dimness of the room, he took a table in a corner, away from the bar. Four hands from across the badlands relaxed at a table across the room, slapping cards on the table, laughing at each other's jokes. Besides the four, the bartender and a bald man in his fifties whom Quay did not know, no one else was in the cantina.

Quay ordered a handsome steak and watched the late afternoon crowd gather. There were two dozen men in the place, and Quay was halfway through his steak when the batwings slammed open and three more walked in. All were heavily armed. One wore a huge Mexican sombrero, though he was clearly American. His most prominent feature was a waxed mustache that curled into circles at both ends. But his eyes, when he glanced around the room, were filled with cruelty. He was not a large man, standing under six feet. His short coat partly covered the silk sash around his waist, and his boots were adorned with huge Mexican spurs. The rowels, Quay thought, were as cruel as the man's face. On his hips, he wore two forty-fives, nickel-plated with ivory handles, expensive weapons, Quay could tell.

The other two men were nondescript, dressed in cowhand garb with dirty felt hats. Each wore two pistols and one carried a Winchester.

They stepped to the bar, the fancy dresser's spurs ringing in the silence that had fallen across the room. Clearly, this was a man who was known and held in awe, if not respect.

"Whiskey!" the man said loudly to the bartender, sweeping his arm around the room. "Whiskey for everyone!"

Happily, the bartender began refilling glasses, those at the bar first and then those at the tables. He placed a shot glass on Quay's table, filled it, and returned to the bar.

"Gentlemen," the sombreroed man said, raising his glass, "to profitable times."

Quay left his glass on the table and continued to eat, staring at his plate, ignoring the man. The room suddenly grew quiet and Quay looked up. The man stood before him, one hand holding his still-filled glass.

"Perhaps you did not hear me," the man said softly, his eyes ugly. "Drink up."

"I'm sorry," Quay said. "I heard you, but I don't drink."

"Do you hear that?" the man thundered, looking about the room. "This man does not drink." He turned back to Quay. "When I say drink, you drink."

"Sorry," Quay said, calling on a resolve he did not know he had. "It makes me sick."

"Sick! Sick! You get sick drinking with the Clodhopper!"

Quay looked at the man sharply and his stomach flip-flopped.

Suddenly, the Clodhopper's features softened, though the cruelty in his eyes may have increased.

"Bartender," he spoke over his shoulder, loud enough for the room to hear. "Bring this man a glass of goat's milk."

The bartender hurried out of the room and returned momentarily with a glass of milk. He placed it before Quay, then moved swiftly away, back to his station behind the bar.

"Drink it," the Clodhopper commanded.

Quay looked around the room, then at Hopper's grinning face. He did not want trouble; he did not want to fight this man — he was too tired. Fighting now would accomplish nothing. Anyway, he was unarmed. He didn't think he would have pulled a gun if he had had one.

Shrugging, Quay lifted the glass to his mouth and drained it.

"Thanks," he said, "that's good milk. May I have another glass?"

Hopper stared at him with widening eyes, then burst into laugher.

"Bartender," he shouted, "bring my friend anything he wants. I will pay."

He clapped Quay on the shoulder and walked back to his place at the bar. To a man, the room sighed with relief. Hopper continued to chuckle, saying something to his friends and glancing back at Quay.

Quay felt no humiliation; only a sense of triumph.

Into this defused scene walked Curly Ford. Looking around the room, he spotted Quay and made his way to Quay's table, taking a chair.

"How's it going?" he asked, and Quay laughed.

"Very well," he said. "The man at the bar just forced me to drink a glass of goat's milk."

Curly looked at the man. "The Clodhopper?"

"He wanted me to drink with him," Quay said, "and I refused his whiskey."

BOB TERRELL

"If you don't mind, then," Curly picked up the whiskey and looked toward the bar where Hopper and his two companions stared at him. He raised the glass to Hopper in a gesture of thanks, and drank the whiskey.

Hopper howled with laughter, and Curly motioned to the bartender to refill the glasses of Hopper and his friends.

Curly could feel the tension that remained in the room.

"You were lucky," he said. "Hopper's a bad one, and one of them hombres with him is Jinglebob McShane. He's a California gunman who's been hanging out in Colorado. Not really a bad sort, I hear, but fast as greased lightning with that gun. He beat Sutherland Bean, the Colorado gunman, and killed him.* They tell me he's not too particular who he points it at, either. I don't know the other gent."

"Oh, well," Quay said, and then he changed the subject: "I take it you're ready for the drive."

"We're ready," Curly said. "We're throwin' about seven hundred head into the herd, and sendin' a couple more boys along. I'm going. So are Sheep and Gus. You comin'?"

"Yeah. I'm going to sleep a while and head out early."

"Make it real early," Curly said. "They're movin' out from the Tumbleweed about four. The Lazy G will throw in when they come by and drive straight to the Willet place. I suppose you'll be there?"

"I'll be there," Quay confirmed. "What time will the herd get there?"

"Shouldn't be later than seven or eight. It's not far. The Tumbleweed cows are bunched on the south side of their range. All they got to do is get em' movin' good and they'll be pickin' up the Lazy G's; then it's only an hour or so to the Willet herd."

"Thanks," Quay said, and started to rise, but a commotion at the bar arrested him. He turned to see the Clodhopper backing away from the bar with his hands poised over the ivory grips of his six-guns, facing the unknown man he had brought into the bar. Jinglebob McShane backed out of the line of fire.

"You damned Jayhawker," the other man hissed at Hopper. "You expect me to pay for th' drinks you ordered for everybody. You're tight as Dick's hatband, you bloody bastard! You've stuck me the last time!" He went for his gun.

Hopper beat him to the draw. He had his left-hand gun out and smoking before the other's pistol cleared leather. The shot took the man in the throat, and he fell backward,

* See *Trouble on his Trail* by Bob Terrell, also published by Alexander Books

135

gagging and clawing at his neck. Hopper pumped two more slugs into the downed body, which gave a jerk and became still, blood leaking into the sawdust on the floor.

"You're welcome to whatever he's got in his pockets," Hopper said to the bartender, who nodded agreement and watched Hopper stalk out, with McShane eyeing the crowd closely as he trailed him.

"Fallin' out amongst thieves," Curly avowed. "I don't reckon anybody'll cry over this one."

"But he killed his own man," Quay protested.

"He killed him because the man was right," Curly chuckled. "Clodhopper's probably got the first dollar he ever stole. He ain't one to spend money when he can lay the bill on somebody else."

Quay left the Cantina trying to grasp a fleeting thought. Something said in the saloon had registered momentarily in his mind as important, but as quickly left him. He *was* tired. Glancing up and down the street in the gathering darkness, he saw no sign of Hopper and McShane; so he hurried across the street and entered the hotel. It was nine o'clock by the clock in the lobby.

He strode to the desk and greeted a clerk wearing a green eyeshade.

"Good evening," the clerk said. "May I help you?"

"You going to be up all night?" Quay asked.

"Oh, yes, sir."

"Then wake me at three."

"Yes, sir, Mr. Quay. Three a. m." He made a note of it on a pad beside the ledger.

Two coal oil lamps dimly lighted the hallway on the upper floor of the two-story hotel. Quay made his way down the hall, the wooden floor squeaking all the way under his weight. His room was third from the far end where a door opened to an outside stairway. The door of his room opened inward. Caution overcame him as he neared the room, and he halted beside the door, gently turned the knob, and threw the door open.

Nothing happened. Moving swiftly inside the room, he stepped to the side and flattened himself against the wall.

All was quiet. He lit the lamp on a table beside him, and saw that the room was empty. I'm getting jumpy, he thought. So much had happened to him these last few days it was little wonder his nerves were frayed. He closed and locked the door and shoved a chair under the knob to brace it.

In the light of the lamp, he gathered up the saddle and his rifle and put them beside the door. Removing the forty-four from the saddlebag, he hung it on the post of the bed, then undressed, and blew out the lamp. Before he went to bed, he padded silently across the room and peered out into the street, searching it quickly in both directions. Nothing was out of place. Two cowhands walked up the opposite boardwalk, apparently heading for the cantina. Three horses were hitched before Carter's Saloon down the street, and a half-dozen stood in front of the cantina. He saw nothing out of the way; so he went to bed.

He couldn't get to sleep immediately. A new thought nagged at him. He had thought Rattler Baines was the root of the trouble on the range but now he wasn't sure. The Clodhopper had not been in the picture before, except as a passer-by. But here he was, big as life and out in the open. There were now two antagonists. Which one was behind the trouble? He knew Baines was involved. He did not know Claude Hopper was, though he suspected him to be. Could they be working together? Possibly, but each seemed to be too big an operator to take orders from another. Still, he had to consider the possibility. He would ask the deputy.

What was it that had been said in the saloon that he thought had bearing on everything? What was it? He was too tired to remember. Perhaps in the morning.

With a troubled mind, he finally went to sleep.

It seemed that he was almost instantly awakened. His eyes snapped open, and he lay still until he figured out where he was. He had dreamed of a gigantic spider weaving a web about him, and he shuddered in the darkness. His forehead was bathed in perspiration. Fishing a match and his watch from his pants pocket beside the bed, he struck the match and looked at the watch. Ten minutes to three. The clerk would be coming to wake him.

Swiftly he dressed in the dark, strapping the forty-four on his hip. He put on his hat, shouldered the saddle, and took his rifle in his left hand, which also held the saddle by the fingertips. With his right hand, he removed the chair, unlocked the door, and stepped into the hall, looking to his left toward the stairs to the lobby.

A board squeaked to his right and he whipped his

head around. In the dimness, the figure of a man lunged toward him, the light of a hall lamp glinting off a knife blade in the man's hand.

Heaving the saddle toward the figure, Quay leaped to his left. Stumbling over the saddle, the man thudded to the floor. Quay swung the rifle like an axe, putting all his strength into the blow, and heard the crunch of steel on bone. He struck the man's head again, and again.

Behind him he heard a noise and rolled off the figure, gasping for breath, bringing the rifle into line.

"Don't shoot! Don't shoot!" the clerk shouted, cringing before the rifle.

Quay lowered the barrel and climbed to his feet. His legs were unsteady and he propped a hand against the wall to keep from collapsing.

"He attacked you!" the clerk wheezed. "He tried to kill you with a knife! I saw it!"

"Remember it," Quay said. "I may need a witness."

They looked at the crumpled figure on the floor, the shoulder-length black hair, the red headband. The man wore a checked shirt and jeans stuffed into knee-length moccasins. Quay rolled the man over and saw that he was Apache. Blood flowed onto his flat, cruel face. The Indian's eyes flicked open, dark orbs in the dim light, and his countenance held pure hatred. Then he gasped, his features relaxed, and he slumped and was still. Quay felt for a pulse and found none.

"He's dead," he said, shaking his head.

The clerk shrank away.

"Will you see that his body's removed?" Quay asked.

"Well, I. . . ."

"Please!" Quay said. "I can't waste any more time."

"All right," the clerk answered, and Quay picked up the saddle and went out the door at the end of the hall.

Running to the livery with the heavy saddle, Quay called the blue roan, which came at his whistle. Slapping the saddle on its back, Quay began to tighten the girths. As he pulled the second girth tight, he saw the corner of a piece of paper wedged between the back saddle housing and the skirt. He tugged at the paper and it was stuck. Forcing the housing up, he slipped a folded sheet of paper out.

Trembling, he opened the paper and saw that it was a letter. A lantern hung in the doorway of the stable and he moved across the corral and reopened the letter beneath the light.

Dear Garney,

We wait with egerness your delivery of the heard. Take it accordin to plan. With your men in place on the drive you want have no trouble getting the heard. Turn it west around Jacks Peek then south around the malpais. We'll meet west of Tularosa and take over. Pay off there on the 16th.

The letter was signed *Gallarogas.*

The sixteenth. That was four days hence. Figuring three days to drive to Tularosa, the herd would be attacked today!

For a moment, Quay looked upward toward the sea of stars, big, round, twinkling lights in the sky, and he thought: Good old Robert. He *did* find a way to communicate. I knew he would!

Quay had no doubt that he held in his hand the reason for Robert's death. Not for an instant had Quay thought Robert was mixed up in a scheme to commit crime. Rather, his friend had discovered the letter and realized what was going on.

They intended to steal the herd — twenty-two hundred cattle — and drive it toward Mexico! Probably *to* Mexico!

Into his mind suddenly popped the words he had heard in the cantina that registered as important and then disappeared, the words he couldn't remember in bed last night. The doomed man had called Claude Hopper a "damn Jayhawker." He thought of the massed herds of cattle going up the trail from Texas, and of the cutthroat Jayhawkers who tried to steal everybody's cattle. That was it! The Clodhopper was a cattle thief! He was going to steal the herd!

He leaped into the saddle, jammed his rifle in the boot, and left the corral at a rush. Deputy Frazier lived in a cottage on the street behind the sheriff's office. Quay pulled up before the house and yelled, "Frazier!"

He called again, "Frazier!"

Lamplight suddenly came from inside the house and a moment later Frazier opened the door and stepped out, buckling his belt.

"Who is it?"

"It's me, John Quay."

"What's going on? What time is it?"

"It's a little after three. Get dressed quickly. I've got things figured out."

Frazier moved to the side of Quay's horse and looked up.

"Got a wire late today but couldn't find you."

"I know what it says," Quay replied. "Garney is Claude Hopper."

"That's right. Garney Claude Hopper. How'd you know?"

"Hurry! We don't have a moment to lose!"

"Got somethin' else," Frazier said. "There ain't enough money in the bank to rob it."

"They're not going to rob the bank," Quay returned. "They're going to take the herd."

"What!"

"Quick, man, get a move on. We've got to save the herd."

"But, how. . . ."

"I'll explain on the way. Let's go!"

Five minutes later, dressed and armed to the teeth, Frazier strapped his saddle on a big bay, and climbed aboard. Quay turned the roan and touched him with his heels. The horse leaped forward and the two left town at a gallop.

Side by side they rode, Quay telling the deputy of the attack on his life in the hotel, of finding the note Robert Murphy had hidden under the housing of the saddle, and that the gang hidden in the hills planned to attack the drovers and steal the herd.

"Who wrote the letter?" the deputy yelled above the thudding hoofbeats.

"It was signed Gallarogos."

"That low-down scoundrel. We been tryin' to catch him doin' dirty work for years. He's from Roswell."

"Well, you'll get him now."

"Where are they gonna hit th' herd?"

"He didn't say," Quay yelled back, "but they'd wait till the entire herd was together. It'll have to be after it leaves the Rocking R."

They were halfway to the Willet herd when Quay pulled up sharply. The deputy reined in also.

"We'd better split up," Quay said. "That letter mentioned Hopper's men with the herd. We've got to get them before the cows reach the Rocking R, else they'll shoot us to pieces when the trouble starts. I'll go to the Lazy G and tend to that. You go on to the Willet place and tell him to get both of his boys. If one of them is already with the herd, send him on to the Rocking R. Tell him to tell Rodriguez, the Rocking R foreman, that Fairly and Johnson were planted with him as spies. Have them put in custody. Got it?"

"I got it."

The men split and thundered away.

Thirty minutes later, with the pink of dawn pushing away the remnants of night, Quay spotted the Lazy G herd waiting in a meadow. The campfire was to his right and the blue roan turned in that direction. Quay pulled the roan down to a trot and entered camp.

A strange man rose to his feet to greet Quay.

"Howdy," said he. "Light and have some coffee."

Quay surveyed the camp as he came off the roan. Hook Nelson and Benny Satterfield sat at the fire, digging into breakfast. Rooster hid behind the wagon.

"I'm John Quay," Quay held out his hand and the other man shook it.

"Britt Garfield here," he said. "I own the Lazy G. We've got some cattle waiting for a road herd from the Tumbleweed. They'll be coming along any time now, I reckon."

Quay accepted coffee and the cook asked, "How you like your eggs?"

"You can scramble them, if you don't mind," Quay said. He was hungry from rising early and the long ride.

"Mr. Garfield, I know about the drive," he said. "I've just left Deputy Frazier, who is on his way to the Willet ranch and the Rocking R. There's trouble coming with the herd, and you've got two men who are mixed in it."

"What are you talking about?" Garfield asked.

Patiently, but quickly, Quay told him of the expected attempt to steal the herd.

"That's incredible!" Garfield said. "Who among my men are mixed up in it?"

"Joe Davis and Spider Wellman," Quay said. "They're in league with the Clodhopper or Rattler Baines. Maybe both."

"You're sure about this? I've noticed nothing wrong with those men."

"They're notorious cattle-rustlers and killers," Quay shot back. "Ask any cowhand on the plains. Arapaho Joe has been described to me as a shorthorn killer from Texas, mean as a snake, and hell on wheels with a gun. Spider Wellman is the same, and they're in this up to their eyeballs."

"I feel I should have some official notification," Garfield said.

"If you wait for that, you could lose your herd," Quay answered. "If we move now, we can stop this thing."

"I don't know."

"Are they going on this drive?"

"Yes."

"I'll bet they volunteered."

"They did," Garfield was beginning to look worried. "Both of them."

"Where are they now?"

"They're out with the herd."

"Can you send these men out and have them come in?" he asked, nodding toward Nelson and Satterfield, "without arousing suspicion."

"Certainly."

"Anybody else here?"

"Just Rooster."

"Send him, too, and relieve another man or two to come in with them."

"We can do that."

"Hook," Quay turned toward the cowhand, "try to warn the others coming in of what we're doing. We'll take Davis and Wellman alive if we can."

"Come on, Rooster," Nelson called toward the chuck wagon, and Rooster scratched himself under his arms and began to crow.

When the three rode away, Quay turned to Garfield. "I'll stay out of the way until you confront them," he said, "and I'll keep them covered with a rifle."

"I don't know if we're doing the right thing."

"Deputy Frazier believes we are."

"I suppose we could hold them for him."

"You'll have to tie them and take them along to the Willet place," Quay said. "Frazier can deal with them there."

"All right."

"There's another thing, Mr. Garfield," Quay said. "You'll need to send someone back to the ranch to bring every hand you've got. This gang will hit the herd soon after it leaves the Rocking R, and we'll need every man we can get to hold the cattle and fight off the rustlers."

"I'll send one of the men back."

Horses approached the fire and Quay stepped behind the wagon.

Davis and Wellman rode up with Clingman Seltry and Melvin Wayman, both of whom were handy with firearms, Quay knew.

When the riders dismounted and had dished up their own breakfast, Davis and Wellman seated themselves on the wagon tongue and began to eat, tin plates resting on their laps. Garfield stepped up.

"Gentlemen, I'm afraid we're going to have to hold you for the authorities," he said.

Davis's plate clattered to the ground and he rose, reaching for his six-gun. But he heard the click of Quay cocking his rifle behind him, and realized he was staring into the drawn weapons of Seltry and Wayman.

"Tie them up, boys," the shaken Garfield ordered. "We'll deliver them to the deputy at the Willet place."

"Will the Tumbleweed have any new hands on this drive?" Quay asked.

"No," Wayman answered immediately. "They've got three old hands coming. That's all."

"Do you know them?"

"They've been on the ranch six, eight years. They're all right."

"Good. Then we can take these two along without expecting trouble from the Tumbleweed riders."

Minutes later, Rooster rode back into camp. Climbing off his horse, he crowed loudly, scratched himself, and said, "They comin'."

"Get the wagon hitched," Garfield said. "The rest of you get mounted. We'll throw in with the others and be on our way. Mr. Quay, perhaps you'd better ride herd on the prisoners."

"Sorry," Quay said. "I'm going ahead to see what I can do up there."

He rode hard for an hour before spotting the Willet herd. Frazier was there. The three Willets were present, armed to the teeth. And Pearl stepped out to greet him.

"Hello, Quay," she called.

"Pearl, what are you doing here? You can't go?"

"I'm not going," she said. "I'll return home when the herd moves. Zeb and Ray are going with Father."

"But you'll be alone," Quay protested.

She laughed. "That's all right. I've been home alone before. Besides, the danger will be with the herd."

Quay knew she was right and didn't argue. He told them what had transpired at the Lazy G.

"The deputy went ahead to the Rocking R," Willet said. "I reckon they'll be out in force when we get there."

An hour later the herd arrived, and the Willets threw their five hundred head in with the rest. Quay kissed Pearl and she mounted her pinto and rode toward the ranch.

"Lordy, that's a bunch of cows," Zeb Willet said, looking at the long string of cattle filing past.

"Fifteen hundred head now," Quay returned.

The Willet cattle meshed in with the others in short order and amid the whoop and whistle of the cowhands the herd moved along smartly. Garfield rode over to Quay and demanded that he be relieved of the prisoners.

"Hang onto them till we get to the Rocking R," Quay said. "Frazier is there."

Quay had never seen anything like this. The cattle walked steadily, and from the herd came the grunts and bellows of animals and a steady clacking of horns striking together. These were mostly longhorns, and some were monstrous beasts. Dust boiled from beneath their hooves and obscured the walking cattle to the front and rear.

Quay heard Junior Wayburn say they would push the herd on beyond the Rocking R before bedding down at the river. Near noon they reached the Rocking R herd and Frazier rode out to meet them. He saw Arapaho Joe and Spider Wellman bound in their saddles and chuckled.

"We got Fairly an' Johnson all trussed up, too. Reckon we'd better detail a couple of men to take these four back to Reynaldo. I want them out of the way when the shootin' starts."

Wayburn singled out Larry Cook of the Lazy G and Slim Williams of the Rocking R to escort the four prisoners back to town and lock them in Frazier's jail. As they rode away with the prisoners, Wayburn and Fernandez pulled soft, knotted ropes from their saddlebags, spaced themselves twenty feet apart, and Wayburn ordered the Rocking R hands to drive the Rocking R cattle slowly between them. Each counted cattle as they passed, untying knots for every twenty head that passed, and beyond the counting area, other Rocking R cowboys pointed the counted steers into the herd as it snaked past.

When the last cow passed, Wayburn studied his rope and announced, "I count seven hundred and three."

"Same here," Fernandez allowed, and all hands moved to their positions with the herd.

Now there were twenty-two hundred head in the herd. Strung out on the trail, the cattle stretched more than a mile. Quay counted twenty-five riders. He had no duties as a drover, but soon fell to work with the rest. He couldn't have held back the roan if he'd tried. When nearby steers strayed from the herd, the roan dashed over, cut them off, and nudged them back into the mass. Quay gave the horse his head and relaxed and enjoyed the work. He was learning rapidly how to be a hand.

A mile short of the river, the Lazy G cook set up camp. Quickly he built a fire, put on an enormous pot of coffee and began frying steaks. As the herd filtered past, heading for the river to water, the cowboys peeled off four or five at a time and rode to camp to eat.

Quay came in with Junior Wayburn and Ollie Fernandez, the Rocking R foreman. Surveying the campsite, Quay knew it had not been chosen by chance. Forty yards to the west, a hillside dotted with piñon pine and cedar offered cover for a number of men. The camp itself was on a rise, offering a slightly downhill field of fire, but the grade wasn't steep enough to interfere with aim. Two huge pines sheltered the camp.

"Señor Quay, may I see the note, please?" Fernandez said, and Quay gave him the note he had found in Robert Murphy's saddle.

Fernandez unfolded the paper and he and Wayburn labored over the writing.

"*Turn it west around Jack's Peak,*" Junior read, "*then south around the malpais.*"

They looked directly west over the nearby hillside at the towering bulk of Jack's Peak, climbing more than 9,600 feet toward the westering sun, and then looked at each other.

"This is the place," Fernandez said slowly, scanning the countryside with narrowed eyes. "They will hit us here. If they wait longer, they'll have to drive the herd back this way."

"I agree," Wayburn said. "We'll set the ambush here. I'll take the herd on to the river and water it. The crossing

146

is small and it'll take too long to cross to do it today; so I'll bring the herd back here and bed down. You stay here, Fernandez, and pull out three or four good riflemen as they come in. Hide 'em in the pines up there an' tell 'em what to do." He pointed to the nearby hill.

"What if they strike at the river?" Fernandez said.

"Maybe we're taking a chance," Wayburn mused, "but if I was gonna steal this herd, I wouldn't hit it at the river, but here when we stop for the night."

Together they rose and surveyed the terrain. The valley was flat here, although laced with ragged washes and an occasional arroyo. Few trees grew on the flat, but because of the washes, a hundred men could be hidden out there and not be seen by the passing drovers.

"Yes, this is where they'll hit," Wayburn said, sounding satisfied with his decision. "When they see the chuck wagon, they'll try to take the herd here. They're probably out there waitin' right now. And if they didn't already know we're goin' to water the herd and bring it back, they've got it figured out by now."

Wayburn finished his beef and coffee and rode back to the herd.

As the others came in, Fernandez chose Curly Ford, Sheep Calahan, Clingman Seltry, and Zeb Willet as his riflemen. When they ate, he instructed them, "You'll have to leave your horses here, men. One by one, I want you to slip into that wash down there and make your way to the hillside yonder. Take up positions that will give you good cover and a good field of fire to this point. Someone from the rustlers will come into camp, perhaps three or four, to tell us they're taking the herd and to make sure we're out of action. You will cue on me. When I remove my hat, open fire, and don't miss. Pick your targets and take all of them out in the first volley, if you can. We'll help from here."

"What about the herd?" Curly asked.

"Everybody else will be riding double and triple around the herd. At the first sign of trouble there, those on each side of the riders who are hit will converge on the trouble spot and help out. We have enough men to handle them, I'm sure."

Slowly, the great herd moved on past the chuck wagon, and by the time the last cowboys were fed and the last steer had walked past, the leaders of the herd were in sight coming back. Quay had remained in camp because he was not at all sure he wouldn't be in the way during the watering process. Occasionally he looked toward the hillside to the west but could see no sign of the four riflemen hidden there.

He watched the cowboys bunch the herd on the flat, perhaps a quarter-mile or more to the east of camp. Cookie refilled the blackened coffeepot and put it back on a flat rock beside the fire. When it boiled, Cookie threw in a cupful of cold water to settle the grounds, and one by one those at the fire filled cups and settled back to sip coffee and wait. They conversed in low tones.

Britt Garfield, John Willet, Deputy Frazier, and Ollie Fernandez were there. Gus Braswell and another puncher sat propped against one of the pines, talking animatedly. Coffee cup in hand, Quay joined them.

"When will they hit?" Quay asked.

Gus looked into the gathering darkness and at the stars breaking out overhead. "Won't be long," he said. "They'll want as much drivin' time in th' dark as they can get."

All three wore belt guns with their rifles in reach.

"When it starts," Gus said, "stay out of the line of fire from the hillside. You wouldn't want to get hit by friendly fire."

"I pity the man who rides into this camp lookin' fer trouble," the other puncher chuckled. "Can't remember the time Curly missed a rifleshot this close, nor any of the others over there, for that matter."

"Anybody comes with trouble in mind," Gus laughed, "they'll cut 'em to pieces."

Quay finished his coffee, avoiding looking into the fire, much as he wanted to, for he knew it would dull his night vision. The stars were out in force now, huge diamonds in the sky, and the herd was no longer visible. The fire cast flickers into the pines, and Quay couldn't remember a more peaceful scene than the camp, nor a more explosive situation. All present grew more tense as the minutes passed.

"Keep that fire built up, Cookie," Garfield admonished when the flames began to die down. "We want our targets clearly lit, especially for those boys over there. Maybe they ought to come down in the wash for closer shots."

"I imagine that's where they are," Willet said. "Least, I know Zeb'll be as close as he can. He ain't one to miss his shot, but closing that distance would shore be insurance for us."

"Watch it!" Gus warned from across the fire. "Riders comin' in."

Quay strained his ears but heard nothing. He stared into the darkness and suddenly detected movement. The figures of four riders began to take shape out of the night. In a moment they rode into the firelight and Quay recognized the man called Ranny, and Jim Rafter, both of whom he had seen at the hideout in the hills. The third man was Garney Claude Hopper, grinning from behind his curled mustache, and the fourth was unknown to Quay. They spread out as they rode in.

"Howdy," Hopper spoke. "How 'bout some coffee?" He started to dismount but Willet's voice stilled him with his right leg suspended over his saddle.

"No coffee," Willet said sternly. "Not for the likes of you."

Hopper settled back in the saddle and focused his beady eyes on Willet. A slow grin spread over Hopper's face. "Ain't very hospitable," he said calmly.

"Wasn't meant to be hospitable," Willet said. "Keep yore saddles an' you can turn around an' ride out o' here."

"Now, look, old man," Hopper protested, but Fernandez cut him short.

"No, *you* look," Fernandez said loudly enough for those on the hillside to hear. "This is one herd you cannot take."

"We done took it," Hopper hissed.

"Doubt that," Willet said. "We ain't heard no shootin' nor no runnin' cattle."

Watching Hopper closely for the first sign of action, Fernandez gauged that the gunman was about to explode. Fernandez reached for his hat with his left hand, ripping it off his head just as a volley of shots sounded from out on the flat in the direction of the cattle. With his right hand he swept up his six-shooter and fired at Hopper.

Four rifles erupted from the wash and Ranny, Jim Rafter, and the unknown man were knocked violently from their saddles.

Hopper was on the ground beside his mount, firing under the horse's neck. His first shot struck Fernandez in the shoulder. The second felled Garfield. He got no chance to fire a third time. Another volley from the wash, and one from the other hands around the fire, downed his horse and riddled Hopper. Quay, firing with the rest, saw Hopper's head shudder with the shock of a heavy slug, and his body suddenly went slack, his eyes glazed over, and he crumpled in his tracks, dead when he struck the ground.

Now the thunder of flying hooves filled the night. The herd was running.

Quay heard Willet bellow, "Get mounted, men. Cookie, take care of these wounded."

All ran for their horses, and as they leaped into saddles, the riflemen came up out of the wash and quickly mounted.

"The whole herd's runnin'," Willet shouted. "Let's go — and be careful who you shoot at."

Aboard the blue roan, Quay left in a rush with the rest.

They rode onto the flat, and Willet, visible in the light of the huge stars, raised a hand and pulled his mount to a halt.

"Listen!" he shouted, and the others plowed to a stop and listened to the night. Thundering hooves were going in both directions, north and south, away from them.

The sound of sporadic gunfire also came from right and left.

"The herd's split," Willet shouted. "Let's go north. The river'll stop that other bunch."

Riding hard, the group soon caught up with the drag. The riders moved swiftly up the left side of the herd, intent on helping turn the cattle back toward the ranches from which they had come.

A figure appeared between the riders and the herd, and Quay saw the powder flash as the figure fired at them. They fired in unison at the flash, and a moment later Quay saw a riderless horse running free, stirrups flapping against its sides.

"Spread out," Willet yelled, and each rider changed direction at a slight angle. In a moment, Quay could see no other riders in the dark, only running steers. He pressed the blue roan in toward the cattle, trying to cave in the side of the herd, perhaps to split it in two and turn the rear section in a more easterly direction. Ahead he saw another rider doing the same, and in a moment a gap appeared in the herd.

Quay and the forward rider pressed harder, and the cattle began to swing to the right.

The other rider dropped back. "Mill 'em," he shouted, and Quay recognized Curly Ford's voice. He and Curly shoved their horses into the leaders and forced them in a sharper circle, then back toward the rear, and finally in toward the running herd now on their right — and minutes later they had five hundred steers running nose to tail in a narrowing circle. Quay was amazed that he had been able to help maneuver the cattle into a mill, and he knew the horse had been responsible for most of it.

Curly broke off and shouted, "Let 'em run," and Quay came away from the mill and rode up beside Curly.

They listened to other remnants of the herd running in the distance.

Gradually the sound of the distant herd faded, and the frantic flight of the cattle in the mill Quay and Curly had created began to slow. Finally it stopped.

"Leave 'em," Curly said. "They're too tired to run again. Let's get back to camp and see what happened. We may be needed there."

They rode southward toward the faroff flicker of the fire. On the way Sheep Calahan joined them, and the three slowed as they approached the fire. Before they entered the firelight, they stopped and Curly called to the camp.

"It's Curly," he yelled, "with a couple more."

"Come on in," Cookie called back. "Ain't seen nobody since you left."

They rode in and dismounted. Fernandez rested against a tree, smoking, his left shoulder bound with strips of a white sheet. Garfield limped over to them.

"We're all right," he said. "Fernandez got it under his arm, but the slug went through. He's not hard hit, and neither am I. Flesh wound in the leg. Three of these others are dead, and we've got us a prisoner who seems willing to talk."

Cookie stood over Jim Rafter, who lay on his back, staring at a stout limb a dozen feet off the ground on one of the pines. Cookie hovered over him, rifle in hand.

"He's shot in the shoulder, like Fernandez," Deputy Frazier said. "He'll live — for a while. Reckon he won't live long after the others come in."

"How about takin' over here," Cookie said to the cowboys. "I'll get some grub goin'." He shuffled away toward the fire.

Quay walked over to Rafter.

"Howdy, kid," Rafter said, pulling on a lumpy cigarette. "How's about doin' me a favor?"

Quay stared at him blankly.

"Take that rifle of your'n an' shoot me betwixt the eyes," Rafter said, an urgency in his voice.

"Why would I want to do that?" Quay asked, astonished.

Rafter looked back at the limb, then gestured toward it with his cigarette. "I'd rather not get swung from that limb there," he said, and Quay stared at the limb, meaning sinking into his head.

"Swung? You mean hung?"

"That's it, kid. Come on, do me a favor."

Quay's eyes narrowed. "Maybe," he said, choosing his words carefully, "but before I do, you'll have to do me a favor."

Curly squatted beside Quay, listening.

"What's that?" Rafter asked. "Reckon I'd do about anything. What'd'ya want, kid?"

"How much do you know about what's been going on?" Quay asked.

"Most of it, I reckon," Rafter said. "What do you want to know?"

Quay was silent a moment, looking at the three blanket-draped figures nearby.

"Your boss is dead," Quay said.

Rafter shrugged. "No great loss. Them others, neither. Mean as snakes." He paused and chuckled, "Like me, I guess. I ain't been no angel."

Quay rolled that over in his mind a moment and thought there were no angels out here in the West. Not even himself. In his wildest dreams he would never have thought he could take another man's life without so much as the blink of an eye, and he had done it more than once in the days he'd been in New Mexico Territory.

"What I'd like to do," Rafter said slowly, studying Quay's face, "is trade you my life for the information you want, but I know these others wouldn't stand for that. So maybe we can work a tradeout. I'll tell you what you want to know and you put me out of my misery."

"Were you there when Robert Murphy was killed?" Quay asked, ignoring the request.

"I was there," Rafter admitted. "I was there under orders, but I didn't take part in the killin'."

"Who killed him?"

"Handy Jones done the draggin'," Rafter said. "It was Rattler that shot him. I guess Rattler killed him. He don't miss many shots."

"Who else was there?"

"Well, lessee, there was me and Handy and Rattler."

He thought a moment. "Cling was there, and Sam — he was Rattler's brother. And Ranny and the Apache. That's all. They're all dead now, but me an' Rattler an' maybe the Indian. He didn't come back from town last night."

"He won't be coming tonight, either," Quay said, and Jim Rafter stared hard at him.

"What happened to him?"

"He's dead," Quay said.

"Who killed him?"

"I did."

"You?" Rafter chuckled. "You killed the Indian? What'd you do, shoot him in the back?"

Quay stiffened. "I bashed in his skull with a rifle barrel. He came at me with a knife in the hallway at the hotel."

"I'd believe a lot you say," Rafter said, "but that's hard to swallow: you killin' the Apache. He was tough as whiteleather."

"He's not any more," Quay said softly. "Why did you kill Robert?"

"He found out we was gonna rustle this herd?"

"The letter?"

"That's right. Old Man Titlow give it to him by mistake. Murphy went lookin' for his own mail an' the old man thought he wanted all our mail. He give him the letter for the Clodhopper."

"And?"

"Murphy read it by mistake. He didn't even look at the name on it. He ripped it open an' read it before he realized it wasn't his. When Hopper found out he was hoppin' mad. . ." he laughed at the pun ". . . and then he sent us after Murphy. Took a while to find him, but we come on him at the Willet place."

"How did Murphy get tangled up with your gang?"

"We met him at the cantina one night an' sorta hit it off. He didn't know who we were, and he kinda tagged along. He never took part in nothin' criminal. He was lonesome and just wanted company, I reckon."

"Who killed Titlow?"

"That was Rattler."

"Not the Indian?"

"No. Some other Indian come in whilst Rattler was talkin' to Titlow. When the Indian left, Rattler done him in."

"Why did Rattler kill him? He was harmless."

"Fit of anger, I guess. Hopper told him that the old man had give his letter to Murphy, an' they figured the cat was out of the bag. So Rattler killed him. He don't need much of an excuse."

"Who shot at me on the way to the Willet ranch?"

"That was one of the boys. When he saw he missed, he figured he scared you bad enough, so he skeedaddled."

"How many of your men were planted at the ranches?"

"Just Davis an' Wellman at the Lazy G, and Fairly an' Johnson at the Rockin' R. The others wouldn't hire anybody else. Willet could'a used 'em, too, but he must'a smelled a rat."

"No, he just had two hard-working sons," Quay said.

"An' a daughter," Rafter laughed.

"Who changed the brands on Willet's cattle?" Quay held to the subject, wanting the answers to all the questions his mind had developed.

"Oh, we done that. Wasn't only Willet's cows. We got three, four hundred rebranded from all the ranches. Pretty good herd."

"Where are they?"

"They're penned in a side canyon in Coldwater Canyon," Rafter said. "We was gonna take this herd tonight to Tularosa, then come back and get the others an' drive them to one of the forts to sell."

"The army would have discovered the brands had been changed."

"Wouldn't make no difference. Happens all the time. They just look the other way an' go on about their business. They need beef too bad to be partic'lar."

"Why did Baines kill Grafton Tumbler and his foreman?"

"They happened to be handy," Rafter said. "He thought if he killed somebody from one of the ranches involved it would take attention away from rustling and focus it on murder. He went to town lookin' for trouble and when he saw Tumbler and Radcliff, he had his targets. He knew they always went for a drink before goin' home; so he went to the saloon and waited."

Quay shook his head at the thought. He heard a step behind him and turned to see a half-dozen cowboys listening. Others were coming into the firelight. He saw Willet and Zeb and Ray, and Gus Braswell had joined Curly and Sheep. Clingman Seltry and Hook Nelson stood nearby, listening. Several others whom Quay didn't know were there.

"You finished?" Seltry asked Quay.

"I guess so," Quay said. "I can't think of anything more to ask."

"Then let's get on with it," Seltry said angrily.

Seltry and Nelson pushed Quay aside and dragged Jim Rafter to his feet. Rafter gasped at the pain in his shoulder but didn't flinch.

"Anybody got a drink?" he asked. "This shoulder's killin' me."

"Just a minute, boys," Garfield walked to the chuck wagon and pulled out a bottle of rye. Uncorking it, he handed the bottle to Rafter, who turned it up and swallowed a huge drought. Coughing and spluttering, he finally got his breath and laughed.

"Thanks," he said and watched Curly throw a rope over the limb of the pine. Two more ropes went over, and only then did Quay notice the two others who were tightly bound and guarded by a quartet of tough-eyed cowhands. One was Joe, whose name Quay had learned at the outlaw camp. He didn't know the other.

"Where are the rest?" Quay asked.

"Rest of who?" Ray Willet asked back.

"The rustlers."

"These are all that's left. Some of 'em are layin' out there dead, and I guess some others scattered. Couldn't tell in the dark. Some may be in Texas by now."

Rough hands shoved the three bound rustlers toward three saddle horses and hoisted them aboard. While Gus tied Rafter's hands behind his back, as the other two were tied, three others dropped nooses over their heads and jerked them tight beneath the doomed men's left ears.

Quay stared in horror as the horses were quieted. Seltry, Curly, and Hook Nelson moved behind the horses, whips in hand. Frazier protested loudly, accusing the cattlemen of taking the law in their own hands, and they laughed and shoved him aside.

"We'll handle this," John Willet said. "No need for you to stay, Frazier. You ain't gonna change our minds, and we're gonna give this gang what they deserve."

Quay couldn't take his eyes off Jim Rafter's face. At that moment, he saw undisguised fear on Rafter's features, that and a quiet acceptance of his fate.

"Wait a minute!" Quay shouted, and the three behind the horses lowered their raised whips.

Rafter stared at Quay.

"Where is Rattler Baines?" Quay asked.

He saw the shine of tears in Rafter's eyes, and then Rafter croaked, "He cut out after the boys hit the herd."

"Cut out?" Garfield asked in astonishment. "Where did he go?"

"He went to the Willet place. He wanted the girl."

Quay shouted. "What do you mean — he wanted the girl?"

"Kid, when he saw we couldn't take the herd, he cut and run. He figured if we couldn't get the cows, he'd at least take her. He didn't care about us. He wanted the girl. He wanted her the first time he saw her in Reynaldo. He might'a planned this whole thing just to get her. *Quien sabe?* Wouldn't put it past him."

The three raised their whips again, and Rafter's eyes found Quay's. "I'm sorry, Kid," he said. "You better hurry. Stop him if you can. He's an animal."

Then, as quietness settled over the men, Rafter looked at Quay once more and silently mouthed the words, "You promised, Kid."

Without thinking, Quay tipped the barrel of his Winchester up, and as the three whips lashed the horses' withers and the animals leaped forward, he shot Jim Rafter in the chest.

He watched Joe and the other rustler kick out their lives at the end of the ropes, but Jim Rafter didn't kick at all. He was limp when he hit the end of the rope, dead from Quay's surprisingly accurate shot.

A couple of men looked closely at Quay, but no one said anything to him. They understood what had transpired between Quay and Rafter, and no one objected, not even Frazier, who had turned his back on the grisly scene.

Quay ran to the blue roan. Without a word he leaped into the saddle and kicked the horse in the sides, shoving the rifle in the boot, and leaving camp at a gallop.

Willet and his two sons were close behind. So were several others, but Quay didn't notice. He was intent on getting to the Willet ranch as quickly as possible if he had to kill the blue roan to do it.

Oddly enough, as he thundered along at breakneck speed, Quay felt no remorse for having taken another human life. Seconds later — no more than minutes, anyway — Rafter would have died of strangulation or a broken neck. He had simply spared him the humiliation of hanging, even though he still swayed with the other two from the limb of the great pine.

Quay's thoughts were on Pearl and Rattler Baines. He had no idea what he would do when he reached the ranch, or whether Baines and Pearl would still be there. He didn't even know if Pearl would still be alive.

But he knew that he, somehow, though he realized it bordered on the impossible, would try to kill Rattler Baines!

No. That was poor and incomplete phraseology. Somehow, he thought, he *would* kill Rattler Baines. And strange as it seemed, even to him, a newcomer to the West, a tenderfoot still, he knew he *could* kill the man. He didn't know how, but he knew he would find a way. In his mind, there was a finality about that. He had too much to gain to lose this last fight.

Another odd thought flashed through his mind: *I don't feel like a tenderfoot any longer.*

The great blue roan ate the miles away, gliding swiftly through the scrub, neck bowed, hooves pounding. Quay rode bent over the giant horse's neck, urging the mount to even greater speed. And as the horse strained for his utmost speed, as if he realized the urgency of the situation, he reached the depth of his spirit and ushered up strength enough to add even more speed to his onward rush.

Holding on for dear life, Quay chanced a glance to the rear, but in the darkness saw no other moving thing. He had long since passed the remnants of the herd, knowing that all the steers had been recovered and the entire herd was once more under the control of its owners, and he knew he had been on Rocking R range for several minutes. After crossing the road to the Rocking R, he had angled eastward on a course that would take him, straight as a stick, to the Willet place. There were no fences to stop or delay him between the Rocking R and the Willet ranch.

"Oh, God," he breathed, "please let her be alive." He was afraid to ask for her to be undamaged, too. There was a limit to what he could request.

Onward the great horse flew. Pink now tinged the eastern horizon. As urgent as the situation was, Quay thought suddenly that the final scene in a drama that had begun last winter in the snow of New Haven was about to come to a conclusion on an arid plain in New Mexico and he urged the blue roan faster.

When the horse raced over the rim of the valley containing the Willet ranch, Quay could make out objects around him as they flew past and disappeared to the rear.

Minutes later he could see the Willet house, and the corrals and the barn and outbuildings.

Approaching the gate as the sun tried to break over the crags to the east, he saw a horse standing hipshot before the house, patiently awaiting the return of its rider.

Racing into the yard, Quay hauled in on the reins, and the lathered roan skidded to a stiff-legged halt, laboring for breath, legs trembling.

Quay left the saddle in a leap, forgetting the rifle in the boot. He hit two of the steps, bounded across the porch, his shoulder striking the door, crashing it inward, and as he saw Rattler Baines fling Pearl against a small table across the room, Quay drew his pistol and lifted it into shooting position.

With startling clarity, as if the entire scene were in slow motion, Quay saw Rattler's hands descend to his sides, and come up with a forty-five in each fist. On the rise, Quay pulled back the hammer of his own six-shooter and touched the trigger. The room filled with the deafening roar of gunfire. He saw his first shot smash a picture hanging on the wall above Rattler's right shoulder, and with horrifying certainty he knew he would never get off another shot.

Something slammed Quay on the skull and he felt himself falling. He hit the floor in a heap, and before his senses left him, he heard one more shot — and then silence.

He was stunned for only a moment, and when he came around the first thing he was conscious of was a throbbing ache in the head. He knew he was bleeding, for he could feel blood running down his face.

Loud footsteps sounded on the porch, and men crowded into the room as the second thing came to his mind: Who fired the last shot? The bullet had not hit him. Surely, Rattler Baines wouldn't have missed at this short range. The room filled with people — John Willett and his sons, Curly Ford, Gus Braswell, and Sheep Calahan, Britt Garfield, Hook Nelson, and Clingman Seltry.

Out in the yard a rooster crowed loudly. Rooster Red! He tried to laugh at the thought, but couldn't.

Holding his head, he sat up, and suddenly Pearl was at his side. He looked at her, still trying to bring his eyes into focus, and then through the gunsmoke, stared at the men crowding the room, their tired, dusty faces filled with concern, staring back at him. Probing his fingers along the side of his head, he felt the bleeding gash where Rattler Baines's shot had creased his skull, knocking him to the floor. Blood ran in rivulets down his cheek.

Pearl took his blood-smeared face in her hands and kissed him. Quay stared at her in a foggy state of absolute bliss.

"Oh, Quay. Darling!"

"Daughter!" John Willet exclaimed. He stood beside the small table against which Rattler had thrown Pearl, and he stared at the prostrate body of the gunman lying on the floor. Both of Rattler's guns were gripped tightly in his dead hands, outflung from his body. Blood smeared his chest, oozing from a hole just to the left of center. His open eyes stared blankly at the ceiling, and frozen upon the rugged features of his face was an expression of utter shock and surprise.

"Daughter!"

"Hush, Father."

"Daughter! You shot him!" Willet touched the table drawer from which Pearl had taken the pistol.

"Yes." She raised tear-filled eyes and stared at her father, who lifted the six-gun she had used off the floor. He sniffed at the barrel and winced, the pungent odor of burned gunpowder stinging his nostrils.

"Daughter!" He could find no other words.

In astonishment and possibly a bit of shock, she stared back at him.

"Father," she cried, "you didn't think I'd let him shoot my man twice?"